Forever and a Day

The Lost and Found Series

Kristen Casey

The Lost & Found Series

About this Book

If you read Finding Forever, then you know…never is a very long time.

When Dimitri said that he was never going to get married again, he was dead serious. After all, he had to focus on raising his small daughter Lilly now that he was her only parent. Besides, there was no way he could endure another broken heart like the one his first wife's passing gave him.

Too bad life had other plans—Lilly's new teacher Emily is too young, too pretty, and too untouched by life's darker moments to make any sense at all for him. She's also too perfect to ignore. What's worse is that Emily wants him just as much as he wants her.

If you loved Finding Forever, then you know…you have to discover what happens when never becomes Forever and a Day.

Includes the bonus short story **Forever Starts Now**!

The Flynn and O'Connell sisters have gone through a lot to secure their happily-ever-afters. Now, one weekend and two big milestones will finally bring them all together again—in this sweet and funny conclusion to the Lost & Found series.

Chapter One

DIMITRI FIGURED HE must have been dead to the world when his alarm sounded for the second time that morning. Not only had he not registered the first go-around, but a quick glance at the clock on his nightstand showed that he'd overslept by half an hour. Which sucked.

Most days, he tried to meditate in his room for fifteen minutes before heading downstairs. After that, he could usually work in about 45 minutes of *tae kwon do* in their tiny back yard before Lilly woke up. Time to himself pretty much evaporated after that, since he had to switch gears into straight Dad duty for her, and *man* did that kid ever wake up hungry. And talkative. And happy. And so, so ready to *go*. The meditating and martial arts every morning kept him sane in the face of it all, but only barely. Not being able to do either was going to seriously screw up his head that day.

Out of habit, Dimitri sat up and folded his legs into position, then closed his eyes once more. After only three deep breaths in and out, it was clear the meditation thing was a lost cause—he was too aware of how late he was already running. So, he pulled on a t-shirt and a loose pair of sweats and padded as quietly as he could downstairs. As he went, he tried to concentrate on small things to keep himself grounded—like the way the air felt subtly cooler at the bottom of the stairs, and the way the textures under his feet changed from smooth wood to woolly rugs and back again.

They hadn't had any rugs at their old place in DC. Anna hadn't liked them, preferring the spare, modern look of bare floors. Dimitri hadn't minded back then. Even though it was louder in the house, it was a happy sort of loud—Anna and Lilly's laughter and love reflecting around the rooms until their whole home was filled with it. He supposed he must have been laughing, too, but it was so hard to remember that. When he joked around with Lilly now, it felt like there was a dismal underside to it—a sad nostalgia that he hadn't quite been able to shake.

When Anna had passed, and he'd realized—once and for all—that they weren't ever going back to their old life, Dimitri had sold off the DC house and almost everything in it. The townhouse he'd rented in Annapolis for himself and Lilly was small and cozy and had soft rugs everywhere because, especially in those first several months, he hadn't been able to bear the empty echoing. It had been deafening—devastating. Worse than spending every day in his wife's hometown without her.

The loose board outside the kitchen creaked from his weight when he walked across it. The back door squeaked when he slid it open and again when he closed it. Even though Lilly shouldn't be able to hear those small sounds from upstairs and behind her closed bedroom door, Dimitri knew that she would. She had an almost preternatural sense of hearing when it came to these things. Which meant that—at best—he had ten or fifteen minutes before she scampered down the stairs, primed for the day.

Out in the yard, Dimitri flexed his toes in the grass and began putting himself through a brief warmup and some basic poses. He was rushing, but it still felt good—normal and natural. Despite being competitive in high school and college, he'd given it up for years afterward. He could no longer remember why.

By the time Dimitri had met Anna, he'd been full into the gym and running scene. They'd even run a few 10Ks together before she got pregnant. But after she got sick, then died…well, Dimitri hadn't done much of anything for a while there. He supposed he ought to thank Dr. Mercer for suggesting he give *tae kwon do* another try. On some days, it seemed like the therapist and her bright ideas were the only things saving his life.

Dimitri phased into a more rigorous routine, beginning to work up a sweat in the spring humidity. Any minute now, Lilly would be banging on the glass, begging for his attention. He had to hurry. He kicked, spun, kicked again—then glanced up at the back door. There she was, his feisty little sprite in pink cat pajamas, mimicking him in the frame of the sliding glass door. Dimitri smiled. Her form wasn't half-bad. Maybe he could start teaching her a few things.

He walked over to Lilly and made a goofy face, and his little girl rewarded him with that silly giggle of hers. Even though she was so like Anna, there *were* some differences—and that laugh was one of them. Anna's chuckle had been restrained and throaty, something that he'd loved. In contrast, Lilly's laugh was giddy and unfettered, and she doled it out generously. To Daddy only, he amended—with almost everyone else, she was incredibly shy. And everyone knew she got *that* from him.

Lilly hopped back from the doorway as he stepped through, chirping, "Did you see me, Daddy?" She punched at the air, her pudgy little fists and fierce frown making him smile wider. "I fight like a girl!"

Well, that wiped the grin right off his face. "Fight Like a Girl" had been something of a catchphrase for Anna, after her old coworkers had given her a t-shirt with that motto when she'd taken a turn for the worse and finally had to quit her job. His wife had worn it all through her chemo, and in some fit of…*whatever*, Dimitri had cut up the shirt and framed the words once she'd passed. Then—because he was almost certainly a glutton for punishment— he'd hung it in Lilly's room when they moved here. She couldn't read the words herself yet, which meant that his daughter remembered it from *before*.

Which was further proof it was going to be one of *those* days for him. Dimitri turned on the coffee maker, then stared into the fridge—buying himself time while he schooled his expression. So many "befores" and "afters", every day. His whole life could be divided into those two awful categories, and there didn't appear to be any end in sight.

"How about some eggs for breakfast?" he asked Lilly.

She hung on his leg and swung around so she could see his face. His daughter stuck out her tongue and gagged comically, even though last week she'd been all about the scrambled eggs with cheese.

"Waffles?" he tried.

"No!" she laughed. *Preposterous*, her tone implied.

Dimitri shook himself. Why was he even doing this? Too many choices for a kid her age led to total anarchy, a fact he'd learned fast and well rather recently.

"Cereal it is," he told her, grabbing the milk. That was good—it was an easy and fast enough choice that he might now have time for more than a five-minute shower.

Lilly ponied up to the table without complaint, and Dimitri pulled out her chair. She climbed into it before he could help and kicked her little bare feet back and forth under the table.

"I can has blueberries?" she asked him sweetly.

"Yes, you may have blueberries," he agreed, subtly emphasizing his grammar the way Anna might have done. He supposed she would have, anyway—Lilly had been too young for that kind of thing when his wife had died. As with everything else, it was all up to him, now.

He grabbed a bowl for himself and joined her at the table. Dimitri told her a little bit about what he was going to do at work that day, and Lilly chattered about the baby animal project they'd been working on all week at school. He sent her up to get dressed while he rinsed the breakfast dishes and packed her lunch, then headed upstairs to see what kind of crazy outfit she'd cooked up.

Luckily, it wasn't too bad that day—simply a t-shirt and hoodie over some sparkly leggings. True, everything Lilly wore was a competing shade of light blue—her newest sartorial quirk—but Dimitri wasn't going to attempt any adjustments, not when the time he had left to get ready himself was rapidly evaporating. At least her clothes were clean. No one could take Lilly away from him for that.

He brushed her wispy hair into a reasonably neat ponytail, tossed her a pair of coordinating socks, then led her into his room to she could watch a cartoon on his bed while he shaved and showered.

The fan in the bathroom was lousy, and the steam from his shower turned the space into a virtual sauna, fogging up the mirror and leaving a faint dew on the countertop.

Dimitri cracked the door to release some of the humid air while he dressed and caught the first notes of the theme song for Lilly's favorite show. He sighed, knowing he'd probably be whistling the tune for the rest of the day. And yeah—that was pretty much fatherhood in a nutshell. No room to be a badass when you were walking around town singing kid songs to yourself.

His hair was still a little damp when they trooped back downstairs. Lilly sat on the floor to put on her shoes while he grabbed her lunch from the fridge, and then they were on their way. Her school was only a few blocks away, an easy walk for her. It was a pretty one, too, the road lined with big shade trees and the spring day not too hot yet. Dimitri adjusted his long strides to her little ones and reveled in the feel of her tiny hand in his. He might not have much left, but at least he had that.

"Is today a Miss Emily day?" Lilly asked, hopping and skipping along.

Oh, yes—Miss Emily. Dimitri reached up and kneaded his neck, which had gone oddly tight at his daughter's question. Three times a week, his little girl started her school day with the reading specialist. Miss Emily had only recently taken over from the prior lady in the position, and Lilly loved the young woman to distraction.

Lilly was making much better progress under her tutelage, too. Maybe because his kid seriously looked forward to the mornings she spent with Emily, or perhaps because Emily was a better instructor. Either way, Dimitri wasn't going to split hairs—he was just happy that Lilly was finally getting fired up about reading and wasn't so discouraged anymore.

"It sure is," he told her with a smile. Lilly let go of him, whooped, and executed a funny little victory kick.

He couldn't exactly quibble with her. Even *he* kind of looked forward to reading days. Miss Emily was indisputably young and pretty, with pale blond hair and blue eyes the size of dinner plates. She had a spray of freckles across her nose and cheekbones that made her seem even younger, and she always smelled terrific. She was efficient and no-nonsense, kind and cheerful, and the perfect person for the job.

For some reason, Emily also had a weird way of making Dimitri feel twitchy and ill-at-ease, like his skin was too tight. He couldn't seem to hold still around her. And he really didn't *want* to notice things about her, but damn—Emily's lips and her body were like something out of his wildest fantasies. The fact that he knew that about her, without any doubt, made Dimitri even more uneasy. Like he was some dirty old lecher, or something.

It wasn't like Miss Emily dressed provocatively, either—she was working with little kids all day, for crying out loud. Still, it was hard for a grown man to miss the way her jeans snugly cupped her ass and her hips, or the way her soft, oversized sweaters obscured some parts, but still managed to outline others perfectly.

Unlike Anna, she wore very little makeup that Dimitri could see. But when Emily smiled up at him, it was a like a neon blast of crystalline eyes, long lashes, and lush, kissable lips. The fact that a guy wouldn't have to navigate past a truckload of cosmetics made her seem disconcertingly…accessible. Her warm, inviting demeanor only added to the impression.

Which was wrong and bad, because his kid's teacher was off limits for so *many* reasons. Among other things, Emily was too young, too innocent, and too important to Lilly's well-being. Dimitri wished sometimes that he could slap some dorky glasses on her, maybe get her to stop washing that slightly messy hair for a week or two. He could cocoon Emily in some grandma clothes and spritz her with mothball scent, and then he could move on.

If Miss Emily weren't so all-fired enticing, then Dimitri might quit noticing irrelevant details about her, and get back to focusing on what was important—which was Lilly, and Lilly's happiness. And…that was about it. His daughter was all he had, and all he needed.

Dimitri blinked. It was a noble sentiment. Right and good, considering he was currently all *Lilly* had. Except, that wasn't entirely true, was it? Lilly had school and friends and playgrounds and her abiding love of ducks—both stuffed and real. She had take-out pizza on Friday nights, Sunday morning pancakes, and the hope that she might get a surprise cupcake here and there.

They approached the tall wrought-iron gates of school, flung wide for the day ahead. His daughter drifted back to grip his hand again, her previous exuberance tempering into a sort of quiet resolve. He wished it wasn't that way, but at least she didn't cry and cling when he dropped her off anymore. After Anna died, Lilly had needed to know he was close—and so he'd given her that, without a second thought.

For the first time, Dimitri paused to wonder if he was getting the things *he* needed, too. He had a throw-away job that he could do in his sleep. Mina was the only friend that he could really stand the sight of, but she was currently thick in the middle of new love and not terribly available anymore. He had his baby girl and the few minutes that he stole for himself when she was asleep, and…his list petered out. Perhaps the time had come for a hobby or two. Even Dimitri could see that his life was looking a bit thin.

He and Lilly made their way across the wide lawn of her school, sticking to the brick pathway that led to the small building beside the kindergarten wing. Which circled him right back around to thoughts of Miss Emily again.

There had to be a way to find out how old she actually was. When he considered the fact that Emily apparently sported a master's degree and years of impressive work experience, Dimitri realized that she couldn't possibly be as young as she first appeared. Despite that, there was probably zero chance a woman like her hadn't been snapped up by some enterprising asshole or another. Looks and smarts aside, Emily was just so goddamn *nice*.

He and Lilly arrived at her door and let themselves into her serene classroom. Next door, the kindergarten was housed in a big two-story space, airy and sunny and filled with windows and nooks for reading and science and art projects. They'd stuck the specialists like Emily in a similar room—still spacious, but more open and definitely quieter. Emily immediately looked up from her desk with a smile when they entered.

Well, there were those glasses Dimitri had been hoping for, but their chunky tortoiseshell frames only made her look cuter—sexy and bookish. Emily's jeans were faded and tight from top to bottom, and she wore a soft-looking black sweater that buttoned up the front. Cashmere, he decided. It had that look, but he didn't dare find out for sure.

In the split second that Dimitri let his eyes pass over Miss Emily, he noticed several things: the freckled triangle of skin exposed by the sweater's deep v-neck, and the little silver necklace glinting there. Her short, pink, newly-polished nails, peeking out below those too-long sleeves. And the flash of more skin exposed at her ankles, between the unhemmed edge of denim and her red suede flats. How she managed to be both excruciatingly appropriate and totally devasting was beyond him.

Dimitri figured he must have some kind of lowered immunity, what with his epic drought and all. At this point, he'd probably find any woman sexy—not just the one who was crouching down to hug his daughter like she'd been looking forward to it for a year. He forced his eyes up to stare out the windows, so he wouldn't check if Miss Emily's jeans were riding low at her back. Dimitri was suddenly, irrationally glad that he hadn't worn his handyman coveralls over his clothes that day.

It hadn't been done out of vanity, only to save time—he'd shoved the jumpsuit in his bag on their way out the door. Since he hadn't gotten much of a workout that morning, he'd worn a t-shirt, gym shorts, and running shoes, hoping he could take a run around the school's track on his lunch hour, if there wasn't a PE class using it or anything. But wearing normal clothes at least made Dimitri feel like he was just another dad in Emily's eyes, and not the modern-day equivalent of the Cockney chimney sweep in that old children's film.

Miss Emily laid a soft hand on his arm, startling him out of his thoughts. Dimitri tried not to jump like a scared cat, but his hand went up to steady him of its own accord, landing on the back of her slim shoulder. That sweater was even softer than it looked. Definitely cashmere.

"Did you need anything else?" she inquired.

Yup, he sure did—a cold freaking shower. Lilly looked expectantly up at him, too, worksheets and flashcards already spread in front of her on the pint-sized table.

"Nope, all good," Dimitri managed. "Have fun, you two."

He reached down to tug his daughter's ponytail—but not too much, lest he mess it up and annoy her. He gave Miss Emily an anemic wave, and then he skedaddled out of that wicked den of temptation. Because, yeah—that was exactly where a dad wanted to leave his little girl for the day.

Jesus. It was nine a.m. and he already wanted a beer. Or a scotch. Or...anesthesia.

At least Dimitri had exactly the right cure for this kind of shit-show. A *literal* shit-show, courtesy of the constantly-clogging toilets in the upper level boys' bathroom. God only knew what the little menaces flushed down those things, but today was the day Dimitri intended to find out. By the time he had to pick Lilly up at the end of the day, his head would be right and tight, and back in the parenting game.

Chapter Two

I T HAD BEEN months since Emily had abandoned her former job in DC and taken this one. Months since she'd gone scorched-earth on her life and upended everything to start over in Annapolis. *Months* since she'd turned tail and run from the man who claimed to love her.

Miraculously, her strategy had mostly worked. She'd gotten a new job as a reading specialist, helping elementary school kids at a fancy private school. She'd made friends with the school's headmistress, Dr. Cecily Thompson, who'd arranged for Emily to live in one of the school's guest apartments temporarily, until she could find something more permanent. And perhaps most importantly of all, Emily had avoided any and all thoughts of the male half of the planet.

Mission accomplished. Pretty much.

There was just one teensy problem to worry about—little Lilly Tsiros's very tall, very gorgeous dad, who dropped his daughter off with Emily three mornings a week. He was lean and long-limbed, with light brown hair that fell in soft-looking waves to his shoulders. He had the most startlingly green eyes she'd ever seen, and it was entirely possible she'd looked up his first name five minutes after she'd met him. *Dimitri.*

He brought new meaning to the phrase "Greek God". Sometimes, he peeked at her when he thought she wasn't looking. Even though he was never inappropriate, when he stood near Emily she swore she could feel the heat coming off him. Rarely, Mr. Tsiros stood a millimeter too close—but it was all she needed to imagine so much more.

Despite her best intentions, Emily had started looking forward to his tri-weekly appearances. Mr. Tsiros—Dimitri—had a heart-melting way of doting on his sweet little daughter. Together, they'd done plenty to lift Emily out of the spiral she'd been in—beating herself up for the way she'd missed all the signs that her ex, Stuart, was a married man.

When Dimitri had dropped Lilly off just that morning, he'd smelled freshly-showered and delicious. For once, he'd been out of his baggy handyman jumpsuit, and Emily hadn't quite been prepared for what his physique would look like without it—tall and corded in muscle, not a spare ounce of flab anywhere on him.

Unlike some of the slicker dads on campus, Dimitri never leered or ogled her—he never so much as looked Emily in the face for more than a minute or two. He was the height of respectability. And yet somehow, she knew he was *aware* of her—tracking her every move, every sound, every breath. She could feel it, humming under her skin whenever he was around.

Which he would be again—Emily checked her watch—in thirty more minutes, when he would pick up Ben Hernandez for his martial arts lesson. She'd been intrigued to learn this new detail about him from Cecily, and it was certainly easy to picture Dimitri doing *tae kwon do*. Now she just needed to figure out a way to see it for herself.

Emily wound her finger in her hair, thinking. Ben made his way down the ladder from the reading loft she'd set up in her classroom and ambled over to sit across from her. He'd said once that he didn't like to do his reading right in front of her, where he felt like she was hovering over him. Instead, Ben preferred to bring his book up to the loft—but Emily couldn't help wondering how much of the time he spent up there was spent gazing out the window at the rolling school grounds, instead of puzzling out the text.

"All set?" she asked him. Cheerful, but not *too* cheerful. The kid was a gangly, disaffected seventh-grader after all, and she could only imagine how he'd shut down on her if she came at him full steam.

"Yeah," Ben replied, his eyes on the table.

"Okay. Work on this and see how far you can get." Emily slid a worksheet in front of him and watched how he clutched his pencil in a death grip.

She wished she could make this better for him. It must have been awful, losing his mother and discovering his school troubles were because of dyslexia, all in the same few months. To have his father remarry and pack Ben off to this boarding school a scant four months later had pretty much turned the boy into an angry recluse.

But…they were all working on him. Every member of the staff that worked with him had made young Ben their pet project. Little by little, their cumulative efforts *had* to make a difference. It would just take time, Emily supposed.

As he labored over his paper, her attention wandered back to Dimitri. There wasn't anything in the rules that expressly prohibited Emily from dating a parent—or another employee for that matter. Heck, the headmistress herself was married to the science teacher, and Emily knew for a fact that the English teacher had a thing going on with the art teacher—she'd busted them canoodling in the coffee shop down the street twice in the last month alone. Besides, she'd never seen or heard a single thing about Lilly having a mom in the picture.

Maybe Emily could slip Dimitri her number? Ugh…*nope*. With a huff of annoyance, she braced her palms on the table. She was getting carried away. Even if Lilly's dad seemed completely different than Stuart, she had no business jumping on *that* party train again so soon. It had barely been six months, and three of those had been spent in a pretty ugly emotional space.

Still, when she yanked open her purse and reached for the lip balm inside, her hand hovered a few moments too long before choosing the tinted one. Crud. It looked like Emily *was* going to do this. After Ben's session, she didn't have any kids coming in until later that afternoon. Maybe she could find a way to tag along and watch Dimitri teach the boy *tae kwon do*. Because that wouldn't be weird at all.

Ben broke into her mental debate with a random question— apparently, she wasn't the only one having trouble paying attention. "Miss Tucker, what is that fuzzy white stuff inside your ice cubes?"

She frowned and looked where he was pointing. Inside her double-walled water cup, several large cubes of ice were floating, and just as Ben said, each of them had a vein of frosty white at their center.

"You know, I'm not sure." A quick glance at his worksheet showed that he'd only made it about two-thirds of the way through. "But, tell you what. If we can get through the rest of your paper before you have to go, we can search for the answer on my computer."

He sighed, "Okay." Not an ounce of joy in sight.

Emily had tried all kinds of books in an attempt to snare the guy's interest—everything from sports to dystopia to sci-fi—but she suspected nothing would do the trick until he got better at some of the tools she was teaching him. Still, Ben hadn't given up, and neither would she. Eventually she would find a story to move him, and then his reading was really going to take off.

The front door swung open right as they finished the last question on the worksheet.

"Here we are!" Cecily sang out. Dimitri's tall frame loomed up behind her, and Ben's wary eyes went round. It seemed he wasn't expecting this.

The newcomers walked over and smiled down at them. Emily stood quickly, to buy the kid a minute to recover.

She held out her hand. "Mr. Tsiros," she said politely.

Dimitri's grip was firm. "Miss Tucker," he responded, low and equally proper.

She thought maybe there was the faintest glimmer of a smirk on his full lips, but it was impossible to be sure. Cecily looked back and forth between them—and seemed about to say something—when Ben piped up.

"You two *know* each other?"

"Sure," Dimitri said. "My daughter Lilly benefits from Miss Tucker's expert assistance three mornings a week."

"Oh," Ben muttered, visibly relaxing. "What are you guys…um, doing *here?*"

Cecily smiled. "I came to see if Miss Tucker wanted to have lunch with me today."

"And *I* figured I'd meet you here instead of waiting at the gym," Dimitri chimed in. "It's such a nice day—I thought we could have our lesson outside on the lawn, instead of being cooped up inside."

"Do we have to?"

Ben was obviously conflicted. While it was clear he idolized Dimitri, even Emily could tell he'd rather die than have any of his friends spot him getting a *tae kwon do* lesson. He didn't want them to know he came to see Emily, or that his mother had died, or that he saw Cecily's therapist sister—Dr. Claudette Mercer—once a week, either. All he really wanted was to be a normal kid—whatever that was.

"No. Of course not. It was just a thought," Dimitri demurred. "Let's just hit the gym. You ready?"

"Yeah," Ben said. To Emily, he asked, "Is that okay?"

"Of course. I'll see you on Friday," she replied. "But…where's your book? Don't you want to take it with you, so you can read a few more pages later?"

Ben's cheeks turned a little pink, and he pointed. "I think I left it up in the loft."

Emily nodded and blurted out, "Why don't I go get it?" before she realized quite what she was saying. Cecily's alert expression had Emily feeling totally off-kilter, and now she was going to have to climb up a ladder and crawl around a kids' loft in front of the man she had a crush on. *Not cool.*

Emily got up there as efficiently as she could. She crawled around the loft, fishing for Ben's small book among the stuffed animal "reading buddies" and big pillows that littered the space. Back on ground level, Dimitri leaned against the wall next to the ladder to wait, and Cecily chatted up Ben about his classes.

Emily peeked at Dimitri, pushing his hand through his hair to get it off his forehead. He still wore the faded t-shirt he'd had on that morning, but instead of gym shorts and sneakers he'd changed into worn blue work pants and round-toed boots. Presumably, he and Ben had gear they could change into in the locker room. Would Dimitri wear a classic martial arts uniform, she wondered, or just throw on shorts again?

The elusive book finally turned up, wedged between the window ledge and the frame of the loft. Emily shifted over to climb down the ladder and watched Dimitri jump to assist her. She held her breath as she stepped down, waiting for the feel of his large hands on her waist, but it never came. Instead, Dimitri hung back a step, and simply watched her descend.

About half way down, he grabbed the side of the ladder and murmured something to her, too quietly for Emily to hear. Without thinking, she leaned closer—and had to slip an arm around Dimitri's back to keep from falling. It was too familiar a gesture, and that was *before* her fingertips accidentally brushed along the sliver of warm, silken skin between the hem of his t-shirt and the waistband of his work pants.

His breath hitched. Emily breathed in, she catching the crisp male scent emanating from his clothes in her lungs. She fought not to relax into the intimate embrace, knowing she had to pull back immediately, when he cleared his throat and spoke again.

"Hand me the book," Dimitri reiterated, louder this time.

He gestured with his other hand, and she spotted the thick gold band on his ring finger. Emily went stiff, hopped off the last few rungs of the ladder, and shoved Ben's book at him. How had she never noticed Dimitri wore a wedding ring before?

She knew her whole demeanor had to have changed, because all three of the people in that room were looking at her like she'd lost her goddamn mind. In a panic, Emily tersely took her leave, and slipped out the door Dimitri had come in by. She ducked into the side entrance of the kindergarten wing, made her way blindly through the halls and corridors, and trotted the whole length of the long building before exiting out onto the rolling green lawn on the other side of campus.

Not again. This could *not* be happening again. She walked down the winding brick path, past huge old leafy trees, and finally arrived at her guest lodgings. Once she'd closed herself inside the tiny vintage kitchen, her cell pinged, and she saw that it was Cecily.

Emily connected the call with a shaking finger. "Hey," she said.

"So…you took off," the other woman commented.

"Yeah. Sorry about that. I received a little unexpected information."

Cecily clicked her tongue. "Listen—I just dropped Ben off at the gym and I wanted to warn you that Dimitri is on his way to see you."

"What!" she cried.

The other woman continued, unperturbed, "I'm not sure if you're inclined in that direction but if so, you won't find a nicer, better man than Dimitri. And for the record, he's very, very single. His wife died three years ago."

"But…" Emily stammered, "The wedding ring?"

"I think it's a total oversight. I guess he just forgot to ever take it off."

"Are you sure?"

"Very. I wouldn't lie to you, not after what you went through."

Emily considered that. "Cecily, I know you're not trying to fix me up with one of the parents, right?"

"Well, technically, Dimitri is also on staff."

"Oh my God."

"Come on. What's wrong with it? I like you. I like him. I can totally see you two together. It's easy!"

"I…" She clutched her phone. "…don't know what to say."

"Nothing to say. You guys will do whatever you're going to do, but at least when that happens, you'll have all the pertinent information."

Emily groaned, and rubbed her eyes. She took a few moments to digest what Cecily had said, then added it to what she already thought she knew about Dimitri. A more complete picture of him was beginning to form.

For example, she'd occasionally had parents ask her if she did any babysitting in her off-hours. Emily might have taken that as a compliment on the way she dealt with their kids if it had been the hyper-organized moms with their planners and calendar apps asking her the question.

Instead, it was usually the dads—a little too slick, a little too smiley, and a lot too much like Stuart for her liking. Emily had always declined, but might she have done the same if Dimitri had been the one asking? As it turned out, he might be the only one who could actually use her help. Not that she could see him ever admitting that.

Emily thought once more about his size, and that impossibly soft skin on his back. She knew her fingers had brushed against him, feather-light, longer than they should have today. But she hadn't been able to resist stealing an extra second of the sensation and prayed Dimitri hadn't noticed.

She imagined sliding her hand all the way under the back of that t-shirt of his—or worse, around his front and across his stomach. Dimitri was lean and broad-shouldered, with long, strong legs, and arms strapped with muscle. His abs would be like everything else, Emily supposed, taut and hard.

What did she want to *do*, though? He was a semi-recent widower, a single dad, and a janitor. He'd never asked for her help, and never tried to proposition her. She didn't know what all that said about him and wasn't sure it mattered.

Cecily's sudden question broke through her thoughts. "Does this mean you don't want to get lunch?"

Emily rolled her eyes. "I do, but only if it's pizza. I've had a fright I need to get over."

"Like I'd say no to that. I'll meet you at Carlo's in fifteen, okay?"

"All right."

Afterward, on the way back to her classroom, Emily could hit the library. She'd had a moment of inspiration, based on how Ben had gazed up at Dimitri earlier. The next book she gave him was going to be about ninjas and dragons and samurai heroes, and it was going to be the key to unlocking all his potential. She could feel it.

Chapter Three

DIMITRI HADN'T EXPECTED to be marooned in Miss Tucker's classroom, and especially not with curious onlookers. It had seemed like such a clever idea, meeting Ben there so he could grab another glimpse of the beautiful teacher. But he'd been ambushed by Emily's sudden, white-hot reaction to him, and even more by her abruptly chilly departure.

Only seconds before, he had been lost—the sensation of her fingers trailing across the sensitive skin of his back jolting through him like a bolt of lightning. Dimitri wasn't even sure Emily knew she had done it, and he felt a little sheepish to be attaching such earth-shattering importance to such a small, inconsequential thing.

After she took off, he just stood there blinking in confusion while Dr. Thompson examined him from over the rim of her cat's-eye glasses. He met her gaze and shook his head, confused. *He* didn't know what had just happened, but Cecily sure seemed to.

With a knowing expression, she held up her own hand, waggled her fingers to make sure he spotted her diamond wedding rings, then jerked her chin at him. *Pointedly.* Dimitri blinked stupidly a few more times before he looked down at his own hand, holding Ben's thin hardcover book—and at the wide gold band on that hand, shining like a warning beacon in the sunny room.

Damn. Emily must have seen it and assumed—understandably so—that he was still a married man. And if she thought that, she probably also thought he was some kind of asshole, flirting with the new girl on campus like a total dickwad. He spun on his feet toward the door.

"What's, um…what's going on?" Ben asked softly, looking between the remaining two adults.

Dimitri couldn't go find Emily, not now. He had a *tae kwon do* lesson to teach.

"Not sure," he told the kid, but then he had no idea what to follow that up with. So, he handed Ben his book and looked to the school's headmistress for guidance.

Cecily jumped capably into the breach. "I'm sure Miss Tucker didn't mean to leave her purse behind. Dimitri, would you mind running it over to her? I can walk Ben to the gym and you can meet him there." She reached into Emily's desk, extracted a lumpy leather satchel, and shoved it at him.

"Yeah, of course," Dimitri agreed, though he had no idea where she'd gone, and therefore had no idea where he was running.

Cecily seemed to understand, though. She whipped her cell out of her pocket and rapidly texted him Emily's contact information.

"Ben, I'll only be a minute," Dimitri explained. "Go ahead and get changed and start warming up in the small studio. I think Mr. Han is in the main gym with the third graders today, so he should be able to unlock the door for you. Okay?"

Ben had ducked his head and begun reading while the adults arranged things, mouthing each word to himself as he struggled his way through the book. When Dimitri spoke, he clapped the pages closed and looked up. The kid only nodded in response, wide-eyed and uncomfortable. Cecily nodded, too, and looked like she understood a bit too much about what was going on.

"You take your time. I'll lock up here," she announced.

Dimitri let himself out of the classroom and walked down the brick pathway, staring at his hand. After a minute, he dropped onto a bench, and probably made all the students uncomfortable while he zoned out and thought. Finally, swallowing hard, he wrenched Anna's ring off, dropped it into his chest pocket, and buttoned it safely inside.

The weight of it seemed disproportionately large. In contrast, his hand felt too light, empty and odd without the ring. Before Dimitri could get too wigged out about it, he yanked his phone from its belt holster and called up Emily's number.

He stared at the screen even longer than he'd stared at his hand, before he could make himself take the leap.

She answered on the fourth ring. Her voice was…hesitant, to say the least.

"Hello?"

"Hey, it's Dimitri. Tsiros. Lilly's dad. Uh, Cecily gave me your number." *Oh, yeah.* He was as smooth as a fine whiskey, all right. It was a wonder he hadn't amassed an entire harem by now.

"Listen, I—"

"It's not what you think," he blurted out. "Will you meet me later, so I can explain?"

"Um…okay. I guess that's…that works. Where did you have in mind?"

"What about…" Dimitri glanced around wildly. He didn't have the faintest idea what might be appropriate in this circumstance, or what Emily might enjoy. His eyes lit on the old stone building across the street from campus, though, and he figured it was as safe an option as any. "What about Killarney's? At eight?"

The little tavern was shoe-horned into a historic building that had once belonged to the school but had been sold off at one point or another. Some enterprising soul had kitted it out as a meeting place for the school's employees and visiting families of the students. Killarney's also attracted residents from the surrounding neighborhood and the occasional day-tripper, but it'd stayed mostly low-key.

It was really the only place Dimitri could think of on the spot, short of dragging Emily to some fancy place downtown and risking coming off as a pompous ass. They'd be able to talk at Killarney's, but it wouldn't give them much privacy. A trade-off, he supposed, in the name of efficiency.

"Sure," came her reply, a few agonizing moments later. "See you then."

"Great," Dimitri said. And then his eyes lit on shapeless sack he'd set on the bench beside him. "I'm sorry—I meant to tell you before. Cecily noticed that you left your purse in your classroom. She gave it to me to bring to you. Are you still on campus? I can drop it off."

Emily made a surprised kind of squeak. "Oh! Thank you, but that's all right—I'm about to see Cecily for lunch. If you give it back to her, she can just give it to me then."

Dimitri rolled his eyes. The headmistress had to have known that, and simply decided to use the purse as a ploy to get the two of them together. He had to hand it to her, too—at the time, he hadn't even realized the doc was match-making. It was impressive.

"Will do," he told her.

He was about to hang up, when Emily rushed to add one last thing.

"Dimitri?"

"Yeah?"

"This is going to sound weird, but when you see Ben, will you pass on a message for me?"

"Of course."

"Tell him the white stuff in the center of ice cubes is actually a bunch of tiny air bubbles, forced there when the freezing water began to form into crystals."

Dimitri found himself grinning at that unexpected tidbit. "Really?"

"Yup, I just looked it up," she laughed. "He wanted to know, earlier."

"Fascinating."

"I know. Never a dull moment with kids, right?"

"You're telling me."

"Okay, well, I should go," Emily said. "I'll see you at eight."

"Sounds good."

He sat there for one more minute, smiling vaguely at nothing and everything, then realized he had a martial arts lesson he was supposed to be teaching. Jumping up, he grabbed Emily's bag and high-tailed it toward the gym building. He couldn't wait to tell Lilly about the ice.

Lilly.

If he intended to go out later, he needed to find a babysitter for Lilly. For the first time ever, on short notice. What was he going to do?

Dimitri couldn't ask Anna's *mom* to watch his kid when was he was going to go out and see another woman. It just seemed odd to consider Claudette, or someone else from the bereavement group.

Truth be told, he really only had *one* option—but unfortunately, she came with a hefty price tag. Steeling himself, he dialed Mina's number as he trotted across campus.

"Dimitri?"

"Hello to you, too."

"Can we not?" his friend griped. "I'm up to my ears in boxes right now. I'm too overwhelmed to stand on ceremony with you right now."

Abruptly, Dimitri recalled the fact that his would-be babysitter was currently packing up her home to go move in with her hot-and-heavy new boyfriend in a couple weeks. Old boyfriend. Whatever—it just meant that the favor he was going to ask Mina was a bit bigger than it had started out.

"So….hey. What are you up to tonight?"

"Packing. As I said."

"You sound like you could use a break."

"Depends. Are you buying?"

"Not exactly. Not for you, anyway."

Mina snorted, and he heard something heavy bang next to her. "I'm officially fed up with you. Tell me why you're calling in ten words or less, or I'm hanging up now."

"I have to go out for a little while tonight and I need you to watch Lilly."

There was a long pause, in which Dimitri imagined the faces his friend Mina was making at him through the phone. "That was seventeen words," she grouched.

"Wait!" he begged, in case she was serious about the hanging-up thing. "I have to meet another person from her school. I promise I won't be long."

"Have you ever even left Lilly before?"

"I mean…I leave her at school every day. And Anna's parents used to watch her when…you know."

"Let me rephrase," Mina said. "Have you ever left your daughter with a non-family member at night before?"

"No. I have not," he admitted.

"Is the other person you are meeting later an unmarried female?"

"What are you, my mother?"

"Need I remind you that I still haven't forgiven you for not telling me about Lilly in the first place? Now you're going to hold out on me about asking some woman on a date?"

"I would've told you about her eventually!"

"*A-ha!* So, it *is* a date!" she crowed.

"Oh my God, Mina. Does this Mack character even know what he's getting into with you?"

"Yup. And he *loves* it," she proclaimed. "But enough about me. Tell me who she is."

"She's just…a teacher at the school," Dimitri explained. "The reading specialist. She kind of got the wrong idea about me being married today, and I have to smooth things over with her."

"Oh, I see. You *have* to. Because otherwise…"

"She's helping Lilly with her reading! If I don't fix this, Emily's going to think I'm an asshole, and not be nice to my kid anymore."

"Well, we wouldn't want that," Mina drawled, clearly not buying what he was selling.

"Mina come on," Dimitri begged. "Can you do it or not?"

"Of course, I can. But my place is a mess. I'll come to you. What time should I be there?"

"I'm meeting Emily near campus at eight. Maybe come at 7:30?"

"Let's say seven. I'll bring dessert."

"Seriously, could you be any cooler?"

"Doubtful," Mina huffed. "Let's just hope Lilly agrees."

DESPITE THE FACT that Mina showed up bearing the fixings for a full-fledged ice cream sundae bar, a package of sparkling plastic tiaras, and a mysterious bag labeled "Girls Only," Lilly still seemed nervous about him leaving.

Dimitri had only managed a quick peek into that bag—spotting a 2-inch thick unicorn coloring book, scratch-and-sniff markers, and glittery crayons—before Mina hustled him toward the front door.

"Take your time," she'd leered, and then Dimitri was alone on the stoop.

As if. He'd had the sinking sensation that he'd be compulsively checking his phone every five minutes—and that was before Lilly had let out a plaintive little "Daddy?" right when the door swung shut.

He'd barely left his daughter's side for most of her life. Anna had been diagnosed soon after her birth and—understandably—hadn't wanted to miss a single second of being with Lilly. Even then, she'd seemed to know she wouldn't live to see her baby girl grow up. It was a while before Dimitri learned why that was, and after Anna died, well…he hadn't wanted to leave the house, much less his only kid.

It was probably time, though. Once he slid behind the wheel of his car, the separation anxiety had mostly passed, and Dimitri realized he felt…free. Hot on the heels of *that*, it occurred to him how much he'd clearly needed this. Even if it was just the one solo night out, and nothing came of the conversation with Miss Tucker—he ought to start taking some more time for himself.

Lilly would be fine. And it would be good for him, too.

Chapter Four

EMILY COULDN'T DECIDE what to wear. She had a vague desire to go with something *more* than her usual classroom gear, but *less* than "knock-his-socks-off." But given the gray area that encompassed, she was essentially paralyzed with indecision in the center of her bedroom.

Was tonight even a date? It was hard to know. There'd been those weeks of hyperawareness, and that accidentally-on-purpose grope of Dimitri's back. Unfortunately, there was also the matter of her classroom desertion earlier—essentially the reason for the meeting in the first place. When she considered that, Emily wondered if she should even bother drying her hair or putting on lip gloss.

Eventually, she settled on a casual blouse that was a touch too short for class and a dark pair of distressed jeans. Her shoes were trickier to decide on. She mulled over the choices: boots and flats, all fairly pedestrian, and mostly screaming "teacher." There was a slew platform heels that she'd favored in college but had stopped wearing around Stuart, because he disliked how they made her taller than him.

As tall as Dimitri was, that wouldn't be an issue with him. But when she put one on, she thought maybe she looked like she was trying too hard. With a disgusted huff, Emily split the difference and settled on a pair of low booties that he'd likely never notice in a million years. They made her feel good, though—current and put-together, and not like she spent her weekdays knee deep in crayons and construction paper.

Emily fluffed her hair, checked that her eye makeup wasn't sliding down her face in the humidity, and touched up her lipstick for the fifth time. By then—somehow—she was no longer too early but running ten minutes late, so she grabbed her purse and her keys and took off up the block.

Dimitri was waiting at the bar when she rushed in, standing next to a stool and watching the door. He'd ordered a beer, but it didn't look like he'd touched it—the amber liquid was still perilously close to the rim, and the condensation on the outside of the glass had already sweated through the napkin.

Out of the two of them, if anyone looked like a teacher it was Dimitri, in his perfectly-pressed chinos and plaid button-down shirt. He was even wearing boat shoes, and he shifted in them slightly as Emily approached. He was readying himself, but the question was—for what?

"Hey! Sorry I'm late," she said.

She couldn't help but notice that he'd removed his wedding ring, since his hand was suspended in midair. And, while Dimitri had raised his wrist, his eyes didn't quite make it to the watch face—hitching instead on her ass and then briefly on her cleavage. By the time he got his stare up to her face again, he was blinking rapidly.

"You're fine. I just got here," he assured her. Over his shoulder the bartender smirked and raised an eyebrow at the clunky lie.

Emily glanced around the mostly-empty room, which was blessedly free of any coworkers.

"Do you want to grab a table?"

"Sure. Yeah," he agreed, abandoning his beer to lunge across the room and pull out a chair for her at a table near the wall.

After they settled into their chairs, a teenaged waitress strolled up, deposited his drink in front of him, and handed them each a large, laminated menu. Emily ordered herself a hard cider and some pretzel bites with cheese sauce for them to munch on, and then they were left to their own devices.

She fidgeted awkwardly, unsure what to say. Dimitri broke the silence first.

"Listen, I'm sorry about earlier. I didn't mean to give you the impression that I was some cheating asshole, or…" he leaned forward earnestly, "Even that I thought you'd be okay with it."

"No, don't worry. Cecily explained everything. And I'm sorry, too. I didn't mean to grope your back like that. It was…an accident." Emily swallowed down the lump that formed in her throat at that half-truth, and then continued, "You probably weren't expecting *that* from Lilly's teacher."

He chuckled. "I wasn't. But…shockingly, I also didn't mind."

"Shockingly?" Now Emily was the one laughing.

"Well, yeah."

"Because…" she drawled, waiting for whatever lame explanation he came up with—and then she realized why he'd said it. "*Oh*. Right. Sorry."

The painful truth hung in the air between them, stifling everything. Emily sat there like a stone, sipping her drink periodically and trying not to watch Dimitri fiddle with the small nub of pretzel he'd placed on his plate. After a while, he looked quickly around and flushed.

"Jesus. People probably think I'm your professor or something. Why do I feel positively wizened next to you?"

Emily laughed. Only a guy who'd been reading fairy tales for the last five years would come up with the word "wizened."

"Oh, come on. You're hardly doddering over there. Besides, you've packed a lot of life into your thirty….something…years."

"Six. I'm thirty-six," he supplied, which was awfully helpful of him. But Dimitri obviously had questions of his own, because then he added, "That probably sounds like a hundred when you're only twenty…whatever you are."

Emily snorted. "You're nice, but way off. I'm thirty-one and haven't been carded in years."

He looked taken aback—he hadn't been expecting that.

"Five years difference? That's it?"

She shrugged. "That's it."

"I mean, it's not like you can't do a lot in five years. Like…"

"Grow an entirely new human from scratch and have them ready to pack off to school?" Emily inquired.

At least he laughed at that. "Yes. As one example."

"It's not a big deal to me, if that matters."

"No. Of course not. It's not like we were born in different centuries or anything." Dimitri's words were casual, but his frown was anything but.

Emily couldn't resist poking him. "Are you sure?"

"Totally," he scoffed.

She'd had plenty of awkward first dates since she'd turned sixteen and her mom and dad had allowed her to start dating, but the one in progress might possibly take the cake. *If* it was a date at all.

"Hey," he said suddenly. "Maybe we should just tackle the elephant in the room, so we can hustle it out of here and move on with our night. What do you say?"

Emily was startled. He couldn't mean—

"I mean about my wife. Lilly's mom. If you were wondering, her, uh…her name was Anna."

Was, he'd said. God, that sounded so final. Emily couldn't imagine having to utter that sentence. The closest person she'd ever lost to death was her mother's uncle, and he'd lived all the way out in Minnesota.

Softly, she demurred, "Oh, we don't have to—"

Dimitri spoke over her. "I thought if you had questions, you know, we could get them out of the way, so you didn't have to sit there wondering the whole night. I mean…if you want. If you don't care, that's cool, too. I just thought—" he stopped. Repositioned himself in his chair. Admitted, "I don't know what I thought."

His discomfiture was so heart-breaking to watch. Emily laid a hand on his forearm, below the rolled-up cuff of his shirt, skin on skin. "Of course, I care," she told him.

Dimitri shook his head. "I know. I didn't…" he winced. "Never mind. It came out sounding different than I meant it. And—*wow*—apparently, I have gotten really bad at this dating thing in the last several years."

Emily smiled. At least one of her questions was answered. Dimitri looked like he was tying himself in knots, and even her meager imagination couldn't comprehend what it must be like for him. First date after marrying—then burying—a woman he'd likely thought he would spend his life with? Lilly's dad was one brave guy.

"How did you meet her?" she asked gently. Not out of any real desire to know, but more as a way to help him along.

"Through friends," he replied, obviously grateful for the assist. "After that, she turned up in this running club I was in, and the rest, as they say, is history."

As he spoke, Emily realized she did have one question she wanted to ask.

"Were you together long?" Like that could measure whether the man across from her still pined for his lost wife or not. Emily felt inexcusably naive, even though they weren't that far apart in age.

Dimitri smiled weakly. "Six years. Long enough to get settled, have Lilly, and then for Anna to get sick."

Emily took a sip of her cider, because her tongue abruptly felt like it was made of chalk. The next part just popped out, without any conscious decision to pry. "What was it? If you don't mind me asking?"

"It's okay. It was breast cancer. Took her in eighteen months. Apparently, the same thing happened to her aunt, but I didn't find that out until it was too late. I might have been able to do something, otherwise—you know, convince Anna to get tested earlier or whatever. I don't know why she didn't tell me."

It clearly still tortured him. Emily said the only thing she could. "I'm sorry."

"Me too," he agreed. "Especially if I could have prevented that kind of suffering."

"How does Lilly do with it?" she wondered.

"Pretty good. We talk about it sometimes, but the terrible truth is, she doesn't really remember Anna. She was a baby when her mom died, you know? If I didn't talk about her—show Lilly pictures—she wouldn't know anything."

Emily fumbled her way through. "It's good that you try to keep her mom alive for her, though. Lilly's so lucky to have you. You're really great with her." More than great. From what she could tell, Dimitri was beautiful and kind and gentle and loving, and Emily could watch him with his daughter forever and never get tired of it. Which seemed altogether a bit much for a first date.

His eyes sharpened as he looked at her. "So are you. With all the kids. You seem to have a real knack with them."

She took another swig of her cider and was surprised to find that she'd drained it. Emily waved at their waitress across the room and pointed at her glass. Dimitri emptied his as well, and ordered another, too.

She told him, "Thank you. That means a lot."

"Do you have siblings? Is that how you know what to do?"

"A couple. I'm the youngest though. I just always got a kick out of working with little kids. Even in high school, I did the camp counselor thing over the summers and stuff. Add that to my love of reading, and a career was made," she smiled.

"Serendipity," he grinned back.

Emily had never thought of it quite that way. "I like that," she said. "A lot."

Dimitri's eyes warmed as he looked her over. "I like you," he told her quietly. "A lot."

AN HOUR PASSED, and then two. Emily and Dimitri dispensed with the niceties of where they were from originally and where they'd gone to school. They exchanged a few words about Lilly's indisputable charm, then returned to the subject of Emily's illicit classroom caress as a way to start flirting with each other.

Dimitri had relaxed considerably, and once he got going, didn't have nearly the problem talking to her that he'd had before. In fact, between his sexy, teasing repartee and the way he kept finding excuses to touch her arm, he had Emily pretty much vibrating like his own personal tuning fork.

Before she knew it, the tavern was shutting down for the evening. Dimitri walked her across the street and down to dark campus paths to her place. At her door, he stopped and leaned his shoulder against the wall, looking down at her.

Emily was sure he would kiss her, but instead, his fingers trailed lightly down her arm and took her hand in his. He lifted it to his mouth and pressed a fervent kiss to her knuckles.

The feel of his lips on her hand jolted her, but he wasn't done. Dimitri turned her hand over and kissed the inside of her wrist, and then her palm. Emily shivered. His lips were firm and warm, and she knew—*knew*—in that moment what kissing him would be like.

But then he did something unexpected. Dimitri untucked his shirt, took her hand and placed it on his back, pulling her closer in the process. His expression was unreadable when he adjusted Emily's hand so that it slipped under the hem of his shirt. And she didn't have to move her fingers far to find skin—the exact soft, warm patch of skin she'd caressed surreptitiously earlier that day.

Now that he had her near, Dimitri looped his arms loosely around her. Emily couldn't decide if he was teasing her for thinking she was so sneaky, copping a feel of him earlier, or whether he'd simply liked how it felt and had wanted her to do it again.

The problem was, she'd had just enough hard cider to feel adventurous, and she had her own memories of touching him that morning. So, Emily slid her hand along his side, then brushed her fingertips along his waistband, low across his stomach. Dimitri shuddered, and she was instantly gripped tight, caged in his embrace. His mouth descended hungrily to hers.

Chapter Five

H E HADN'T EXPECTED how such a simple thing, such a simple kiss, would affect him. In an instant, Dimitri's whole over-sexed adolescence came roaring back—his nerves jumping under his skin in anticipation and his fingers itching to seize her.

The one quick peck that he'd intended, bloomed almost immediately into some serious necking against Emily's door. When that wasn't enough anymore, she managed to get said door unlocked and dragged Dimitri breathlessly into her rooms—where things escalated even more rapidly.

The sudden privacy was like throwing gasoline on a bonfire, and without even considering what he was doing, Dimitri found himself peeling off both their shirts with a grinding desperation.

It wasn't like there was any rush, though. He'd texted Mina a couple times earlier to check on things and had been tersely informed that his television was better than hers, Lilly was sound asleep, and Mina had shows to catch up on. But even knowing they had time, he couldn't seem to help himself—Dimitri was plastered all over Emily like a cheap-ass suit before she could even blink.

He pried his lips off hers just far enough to ask, "Is this okay?"

"*So* okay," Emily gasped.

She tried to pull him toward the bedroom, but with her moving backward and him so much taller, their feet and legs kept getting tangled up, making them trip and stumble. Emily was giggling, and Dimitri was starving—so finally he simply lifted her up and took the last several steps himself.

Hanging onto Emily's lush hips while she wriggled out of her bra, he backed her toward the bed that took up most of the small room. Her breasts—dear God, her breasts. How had he forgotten how beautiful a nude woman could be? Dimitri cupped her reverently in his palms.

Emily arched into his hands, but her own were busily undoing his fly and pushing his jeans down his legs. She was too short for him to get his mouth on her without a lot of awkwardness, so Dimitri used his foot to hook her behind an ankle and guided her back onto the bed.

"Still doing okay?" he wondered.

Emily beckoned to him, tugging at his hands until he climbed onto the bed and covered her with his body. Her lips were too tempting to resist. Her soft hands stroked over the skin of his back, and left trails of fire in their wake.

"Emily?" he prodded after a moment.

She nodded quickly. "All okay," she agreed. "Everything is okay, I swear."

He let his body drop down, until their pelvises were pinned together. Little Miss Emily ground against him so perfectly, Dimitri couldn't help but let out a loud groan. She laughed, breathy and low and delighted—and it was probably the sexiest sound he'd ever heard.

"I want you so much," he admitted between kisses. "I'm sorry. Going too fast." Not like he could stop. He slid down and took the dusky tip of one breast into his mouth, and Emily wound her fingers into his hair so tight it stung. His cock strained against her leg.

"Go faster," she begged him. "Please."

If that was what she wanted, he could certainly oblige. Dimitri fumbled with the clasp of her pants, then shoved them and her panties down her legs in one economical sweep. He shifted back to kneel next to the bed, dragged Emily toward him, and without another word set his mouth on her velvety core. She yelped, then settled into the kind of moans and gasps that made a guy seriously feel like he was at the top of his game.

She didn't let him get her all the way there, though. Far too soon, Emily was pulling at his shoulders and yanking on his arms, until Dimitri had to give up the race to see what all the fuss was about.

Once she had him braced over her again, sweet little Emily did the unexpected once more.

"Are *you* doing okay?" she inquired.

"Are you kidding me?" he wondered. "I'm, like…boldface and all-caps okay."

She grinned, "Would you still be okay if I gave you this?" and pressed a condom into his hand. Where in hell had she procured *that* from? Not that Dimitri wasn't grateful—*he* certainly hadn't been prepared for anything like this.

"Would you?"

"I'm game if you are."

Holy fuck. "I think I am the gamest man to ever walk the earth right now," he told her, panting right into those laughing baby-blue eyes.

"Then get busy, big guy," Emily said. "I'm so close."

Right. Because when a smoking-hot woman handed you a condom and told you to snap to it, adoring gazes were probably *not* what she was after. Dimitri ripped that packet open and rolled it on, squeezing his eyes shut to get past the initial torment.

He didn't think he'd ever been so hard in his life. He was probably hard enough to pound nails, hard enough to…he sank into Emily's scorching heat, fast and deep and true, and lost his train of thought.

Dimitri groaned again, more loudly this time. Emily wasn't exactly keeping her thoughts to herself, either.

"Oh my God," she cried, then seemed to get stuck on that first syllable, releasing another breathless "Oh!" each time he pushed into her.

It gave him the most insanely erotic charge to hear her getting into it like that. He thrust harder, then deeper, and then—when she begged him—faster, too. The rickety guest suite bed thumped against the wall, the two of them were noisier than a cat house on ladies' night, and the whole thing took about four minutes before they were collapsing against each other in blissful satiation.

Dimitri's heart was pounding, and his chest was heaving—and he felt like he'd been wrenched rather abruptly from his darkness, back into the land of the living. It was glorious. *Emily* was glorious. He rolled onto his side to tell her so, when a series of loud bangs shook the wall behind the headboard.

"What the hell?" he wondered.

A muffled voice demanded, "Keep it down!"

"Oh no," Emily gasped, chagrined.

Dimitri stared at her, aghast too. "Does someone *live* over there?"

"I didn't know! I thought it was empty!" she whimpered.

They lay there frozen, holding their breath for long seconds, while they waited to see if the mysterious neighbor had anything else to add. Dimitri watched Emily struggle to keep her composure, but the poor thing just couldn't keep it together.

At last, she dissolved into crying, gasping giggles, and he had to grin too—it *was* pretty hilarious. Watching her mop at her face with the sheets soon had Dimitri chuckling, too. Before long they were at it again, the neighbor was back to knocking on the adjoining wall, and all was right in Dimitri's world.

EMILY WAS, IN a way, nothing new—like every other woman he'd ever touched, including Anna. She was soft, fragrant, and pretty in that way that all women seemed to be. But she was also something else, something unique and intoxicating. An unexplored land not yet conquered—and every competitive, ambitious bone in Dimitri's body felt like it was suddenly intent on winning her.

He didn't manage to extract himself until well after one. He left delicious, enticing Emily sound asleep in her bed—as difficult as that was—and arrived home to find Mina sacked out on his couch. He squeezed her shoulder gently.

"Hey," he whispered. "Sorry I'm so late."

"No sweat," she murmured, sitting up and straightening herself out. "How'd it go?"

Then Mina looked at him. *Really* looked at him. She burst out laughing and held up her hands.

"Never mind," she beamed. And then, more seriously, she added, "Good for you."

Dimitri bristled. "What do you mean? We just…"

She waved him off, pushing to her feet and snagging her purse off a side table. She bustled officiously past him and headed for the door.

Over her shoulder, Mina said, "Don't fight it, D. It's supposed to be fun."

"Wait."

"What's wrong?" She paused with her hand on the door.

"It's just…should I even be doing this?" he wondered. "I mean, what could I ever have to offer someone like her? I'm not in any position to go out all the time, and frankly, Lilly and I are sort of a package deal."

"Somehow, I suspect this chick knows that."

"But Emily might not even *want* kids. Then what do I do?"

"Honestly, Dimitri?" Mina shrugged. "It's simple—communicate. Isn't that what all you parent types are always telling your kids? Follow your own advice and *use your words*."

"But…what if it's not enough?"

"That's simple, too. Then she doesn't deserve you."

Suddenly, he remembered something important. "I almost called her the wrong name," he blurted out, before Mina could leave.

She frowned at him in the foyer. "You didn't, though. Right?"

"No. It got all garbled when I tried to keep it from coming out. Anna's brother used to call her 'Kiki,' and my *yia yia* called her *Koukla*—and somehow I ended up calling Emily 'Kikla' at a very…inopportune moment."

Mina snorted at his insanity. "What did she do?"

"I'm not sure she noticed, to be honest," he admitted.

"Then you're probably in the clear. It was an honest mistake, Dimitri. I wouldn't sweat it."

"Are you…" he hesitated, not wanting to sound like his kid—but he had to. "Are you *sure*?"

"Like I said, it's supposed to be fun. Let yourself up off the mat, dude."

Mina had already been through this weird reentry stage, so Dimitri felt reasonably comfortable asking, "Nothing like that ever happened to you?"

"No, but you probably shouldn't ever use me as a barometer of what's normal," she laughed. "Besides, this wasn't your first time back in the saddle, was it?"

"T.M.I., man," he complained.

"Wait, it *was*?" Mina squawked.

Dimitri could feel his neck getting hot, and tugged at his collar to let a little air in. "It doesn't matter."

"Of course, it matters! Good Lord, why didn't you say so?"

"Maybe because it's none of your beeswax?" Sometimes this woman felt more like a pesky little sister than an unexpected friend he'd found in a bereavement group.

Mina made a *settle-down* motion with her hands and took a deep breath. Dimitri inhaled a breath of his own, hoping it would fortify him for whatever was going to come out of her mouth next.

"All right, listen. You got back on the horse…"

"Can we please dispense with all of the riding analogies?" he begged. "*Please?*"

"Would you focus?" she huffed. "You reclaimed…your…*intimacy*—or whatever you want to call it—and that is a good thing. This woman sounds like a solid, non-crazy choice, and now you just need to give your brain and your heart a little time to catch up with your libido." She laid a hand on his arm and searched his eyes. "Okay? Try not to freak out. Talk to Claudette."

Dimitri had to smile at the way the tables had turned between the two of them. Only a few months earlier, he'd been the asshole doling out sage advice from his impenetrable mountaintop, and Mina had been the clueless new dater. A surge of affection for her rushed through him, and Dimitri stepped forward to tug her into a hug.

It took her a minute to relax out of her knee-jerk resistance but when Mina hugged him back, it was with every ounce of strength and courage she had—and he hated to admit how much he'd needed it. She truly was one in a million.

AFTER MINA LEFT, Dimitri wandered around his home expecting everything to feel as different as he did. Oddly, nothing had changed. All the ephemera of his current existence was pretty much exactly where he'd left it.

Eventually, he ended up in Lilly's room, gazing down on his sleeping angel in her little girl bed. She was the same as always, too—pearlescent baby skin, dark and wild curls tossed across her pillow, and a hint of a frown, like she had to concentrate on staying asleep. The thick new coloring book Mina had brought her was propped on her nightstand, and her kitten nightlight cast a gentle pink glow around the room.

What would Lilly think, if Dimitri told her where he'd been tonight? Maybe not *precisely* where…but that he'd been out with a woman who wasn't her mother? Would she feel betrayed? Upset? Delighted? It was hard to guess. The fact that Emily was Lilly's reading teacher made things so much more complicated.

In any case, it was far too soon to tell his kid anything, anyway. Dimitri might be deliriously amazed by the direction his meeting with Emily had taken tonight, but maybe nothing would come of it. There was no way he could simplify the situation enough to explain it to his little girl quite yet, and if it all blew away like the morning fog—he might never have to.

Besides, Dimitri had an unsteady feeling that come morning, his amazement might morph into an epic state of overwhelm. As he'd learned, it would be better for him to work through *that* mess without the curious eyes of a five-year-old calling the play-by-play.

He'd have to be content with the short debriefing Mina had given him and ride out tonight's endorphin high alone. Well…maybe not one-hundred-percent alone. Somewhere across town, there was one other person who might be feeling something similar to what he was.

Dimitri slipped back into the hallway, extracted his cell from his pocket and fired off a quick "good night" text to Emily. Despite having been asleep when he left, her response was gratifyingly immediate, and he battened down his immediate urge to phone her, so he could hear her sexy voice again.

He went into his bedroom and rested his phone in the charging dock on his bureau. Then, Dimitri stripped down to his boxers and climbed into bed. He could still taste Emily on his lips—could still smell her on his skin—but showering was the last thing he wanted to do. Instead, he dreamed the woman herself was there with him, and prayed that Anna wouldn't mind.

Chapter Six

B Y THE TIME Dimitri brought his daughter to school the next
morning, Emily had worked herself into a bit of a mood. She
was sort of embarrassed—all the man had wanted the night before
was to explain that he wasn't actually married. Needless to say, he'd
gotten quite a bit more than he'd bargained for.

Emily had, too, though. It wasn't like she was normally in the
habit of jumping in the sack on the first date. Even so, she couldn't
quite bring herself to regret it—Dimitri was all that and a bag of
chips, as the kids used to say.

His expression was adorably uncertain. While Lilly was getting
situated, Emily found a moment to whisper, "I don't know what
got into me last night. I *never* do that kind of thing."

"I feel you," Dimitri agreed. "Me either." Then, with a smirk and
a sly sideways look, he added, "Or should I say, *I felt you?*"

Emily giggled, then slapped a guilty hand over her mouth. "You
did *not* just say that."

"Damn. I totally did." He was flushed, but grinning.

"See, that's how we got here to begin with," she accused under
her breath.

"I think it's fixable, though," he said. "Meet me for lunch and we can back this train up and get to know each other better. The right way."

In his deep, sexy voice, that still sounded dirty as hell to her. Emily glanced quickly at Dimitri's daughter, then raised her eyebrows at him.

"Orally," he corrected. Then laughed, "*No.* I mean *vocally.*"

"For some reason, that still sounds bad."

"Completely above board. I promise."

It felt giddy to agree—to give in to the craziness, despite all the reasons why she shouldn't. Emily was beginning to fear she was a goner where handsome Mr. Tsiros was concerned.

WHAT STARTED AS a simple effort to backtrack and shift their relationship into the slow lane, turned into almost daily lunch dates in various nearby restaurants and out-of-the-way spots around campus. Since Dimitri couldn't meet up in the evenings very easily, they strolled around town during the day like a couple of lovesick teenagers—then talked on the phone most nights, too.

Which was sweet and…sort of perfect. Dimitri was charming, smart, and kind, and the more Emily got to know him, the better she liked him. However, now she was ready to get back to the whole "starting things off with a bang" thing. Literally. She wanted—no, she needed—Dimitri to lose control and work his *God of the Sheets* magic again. So she cooked up a plan.

The next time he showed up—dropping Lilly off with a furtive wink for Emily—she was ready for him. While his daughter hung up her jacket and Dimitri sauntered away, Emily fired off a quick text to his cell.

Meet me at my place for "lunch" today?

Through the window, she watched him stop in his tracks, spin back to look at her through the window, and grin from ear to ear. He texted back,

Wouldn't miss it for the world. I love "lunch."

THE BUILDING EMILY lived in was once a dormitory, but in recent years had been fitted out with several guest apartments for visiting faculty and the temporary needs of staff members. It was small but convenient, and reasonably close to her classroom. Emily ought to have been able to get to it—and Dimitri—on time without any problems.

Instead, she got hung up in the kindergarten hallway updating one of the teachers on her student's progress. It took ages to break free, so she ran the rest of the way home. When she finally came plowing through her building's lobby, Dimitri was already leaning against the wall next to her front door waiting for her.

He straightened in anticipation. "Hey," he said. "You're late. I win."

"Sorry," she cried, hurrying headlong toward him before she noticed they had company.

A short, slim man with thick glasses and a ginger beard was standing with his key in the lock of the neighboring door. He checked his watch and glanced between them.

"Did I miss something?"

"No. Sorry," Dimitri blustered. "I was just meeting, uh..." He stopped as if he'd blanked on her name.

"Miss Tucker, I presume?" the man inquired.

"Right."

The other man looked like he would rather be anywhere else.

"Mr. Boggs!" Emily squeaked. "I thought you had the sixth graders for testing this period!"

"I do," he said grimly. "I just came by to pick up my proctor badge."

Emily looked back at Dimitri—he was trying not to laugh.

She blurted out, "He needed to borrow my vacuum," at the same time Dimitri explained, "I came by to check out her A/C unit."

"I'll bet." Boggs rolled his eyes as he cracked open his door. He drawled, "Incidentally, I have twelve-year-olds in my class that are better liars."

Emily felt her face heat and turned to gape at Dimitri. A mortified flush was inching upward from his collar, staining his skin an outrageous red.

She tried to let him into her suite as fast as she could, but she still managed to drop her keys twice in the effort. By the time they made it inside, he was chuckling in that dark, seductive way he had. Two minutes later they heard Mr. Boggs's front door slam, and his reedy voice call out, "I'm leaving now!"

Dimitri nearly choked on his tongue. "*What* is that man doing here?" he wondered.

So much for her effort to arrange a sexy midday tryst. "Apparently it's only for a couple days," Emily explained. "Cecily told me his real apartment is getting fumigated this week."

"Figures," Dimitri muttered. He still reached for her, though, and dragged her in close. "I hope he doesn't expect me to apologize for last time. Or this time. Or any time, for that matter."

Emily smiled. "Maybe we could just write him one note at the end of his stay, to cover everything he's likely to overhear," she mused.

Dimitri dipped his head to suck hard at her neck, then said, "*Sorry our life is more interesting than yours.*"

"*Sorry, not sorry,*" Emily tacked on.

He pulled her shirt off, kicked off his shoes, and urged her toward the bed. "*We hope things pick up for you now that you're bug-free.*"

"*When you leave, don't let the door hit you in the ass,*" Emily finished, pinching Dimitri on his for emphasis.

They fell into her narrow double bed. After some awkward shifting around, trying to accommodate both of them, he began laughing deep in his chest, his mirth slowing down the urgent ardor he'd begun with.

"Is it my imagination or is this the most uncomfortable bed in the universe? How did I not notice it before?" he asked. "How do you even fit in this thing?"

"I fit just fine before you showed up," Emily huffed.

"Right. Because you're…what? Three apples high?" he grinned down at her, pinning her beneath him with his long, strong legs.

She narrowed her eyes at him, kind of resenting the Smurf reference. "Oh, and I suppose you're, like, a hundred apples high, right?"

"Give or take," Dimitri mused. "But seriously, what'd you do to piss off the doc?"

"Absolutely nothing!" She whacked him on the shoulder. "This is the exact same mattress that every other guest on campus has!"

He rolled to the side with a frown, pulling her with him. "Really?" His eyes focused on the far wall, contemplating that. "That just seems cruel."

For him, it probably would be. He did take up an awful lot of *space*, his arms and legs sprawled every which way as he smashed up against the wall, trying to carve out enough space for Emily against his chest. If she were less reluctant to tackle him, it might be easier—she could just drape herself over him and enjoy the way he made her melt.

But this was going to be their first *planned* time together—their first time in broad daylight, no less—and Emily suddenly felt a bit shy. She was a grown woman, no stranger to the act, and she'd invited him there. So why was she nervous?

She knew the answer to that, though. The more she fell for Dimitri, the more curious she got about the woman who'd won him first. He'd loved Anna so much, that he'd married her—had a baby with her. What had his wife been like? Emily wondered again. Had she been prettier? Slimmer? Sexier?

Hell. What did she think she was doing?

Dimitri had no such qualms, though. Completely oblivious to her inner turmoil, he set about using every inch of the limited space on her mattress to seduce every inch of her. Before long, Emily's questions were the last thing on her mind—the enthusiastic man making love to her made damn sure of that.

DIMITRI SEEMED TO be on a mission to make excellent use of their entire lunch break. It wasn't long after their first go around before he was kissing her again, clearly angling for round two.

"Already?" Emily yelped. "How is that even possible? Jeepers, you're insatiable."

His mouth suddenly released her breast. "*Jeepers?*" he laughed down at her.

"So, I spend my time around little kids," she huffed. "That is completely beside the point. How can you be ready for another go so soon? I feel like an overcooked noodle right now."

"I guess you're just that good," he murmured, diving for her chest again.

Emily pushed on his head. "No, I'm not. What's really going on?"

Dimitri relented, rolling to the side but keeping his hand on her waist like he was worried his prize might get away from him. Before, he'd been so happy he was almost silly—his eyes twinkling, and mouth fixed in a sexy grin. Now, his expression tempered into something a bit more serious.

"Why does there have to be something going on?"

Emily shoved at his shoulder. "You tell me."

"All right. Well," he shrugged, "Let's just say I've had a bit of a dry spell. I didn't realize how much I missed all…*this*. But I guess I did. A lot."

"How long of a dry spell are we talking?" she frowned, eyeing him. It seemed inconceivable that he hadn't had women trying to jump his bones at every turn, but he *was* a fairly reserved person. Maybe he'd held them at bay without realizing.

Dimitri looked away and swallowed, his Adam's apple jumping in his throat. "Almost four years," he said.

Right. Because his wife had been ill and then she'd died, and Emily was a flaming idiot to not have considered that.

"You mean you haven't…I mean," she tried. "Not since…"

"No," he stated flatly. "I have not had sex since well before Anna died." After a long moment, he turned his head to meet her gaze. His eyes pleaded with her. "I'm sorry. I came on too strong, didn't I? Honestly, sex was about the last thing on my mind all that time. But now…God, I don't know how to explain it. You're just so—*you*. It's like the second I kissed you, everything came rolling back in this enormous tidal wave."

He swallowed again, and Emily studied him. His cheeks were…*pink?*

"No—it's okay. Don't be embarrassed," she said, shifting toward him. She stroked Dimitri's face. "I should have realized," she whispered. "I just spoke without thinking, that's all."

"You're fine," he assured her. His hand was large and heavy on her hip, and warm in the air conditioning.

Emily laid her head against his chest and listened to his heart thump steadily away inside his chest. She smoothed her hand over the curve of his shoulder, the colorful ink of his tattoo sleeve swirling across his skin. With her fingertip, she touched the trunk of a small fruit tree at the center of the design, its bare black branches reaching out into the rest of the tattoo like tendrils of smoke.

On one branch was a little pink bloom with the letter "A" in script at its center. From the branch below dangled a perfect round peach with a delicate "L" gracing its flesh. A whole tree, with only one flower, and one piece of fruit—such a sad depiction of a life cut short. As detailed and realistic as the tattoo was, it must have been painful to sit through. Wickedly apropos.

Emily's curiosity was a bad, bad thing. She couldn't stop herself from asking, "Four *years?* Really?"

Dimitri chuckled, though. "Didn't even jack off once," he admitted.

"Criminy. No wonder you're insane—you're desperate."

"Not *just* that. To be fair, you also happen to be an especially delectable lunch date."

"I think your judgement might be compromised," Emily demurred.

"I said I had a drought, not a lobotomy," he protested.

"If you say so."

"What about you?" he asked tentatively. "I take it from your horror that you've never experienced something…similar?"

"Recently exited a serious relationship," she told him. "Other than that, not much to tell, I'm afraid."

"Who was he?"

Emily ducked her head to his chest again, in case her face gave her away. "A guy I met on the train. He was older—it didn't work out."

Such a succinct way to encompass the last eighteen months of her life. Her entire recent existence, broken up into oddly-regular blocks of time. Six months of fantasy, hoping she'd spot Stuart during her daily commute. Another six months, in which she'd fallen wholeheartedly for a man who lied as easily as breathing. What came after that was not fantasy, but nightmare. A half-year of wanting, a half-year of blindness, and a half-year of regret to round out the set.

Dimitri shifted so he could catch her eye again. "I'm older," he pointed out.

Five years older, if Emily remembered correctly. Stuart had been three times that.

She said, "Trust me, it's different."

"You really don't want to talk about it, do you?"

"Nope."

He studied her. "He broke your heart." It wasn't a question.

Emily forced a smile to brush the comment off, but it was impossible to tell how believable she was. "No biggie," she said. "It happens."

"Not always," he retorted. "I wouldn't do that. I won't do that."

Emily laughed, and yeah—it sounded bitter. "You can't know that. You can't *promise* that."

Now it was Dimitri's turn to scowl. "I'm sorry you were hurt." Then he tucked one long arm beneath his head and smiled faintly at the ceiling. "Let's say—I'll endeavor not to do the same."

Chapter Seven

ONLY GETTING TO see Emily on his lunch breaks was wearing a bit thin, but Dimitri didn't think he wanted to bring her over to his house *quite* yet. It seemed like it would be hard for Lilly to adjust to it. Seeing him be affectionate with a new woman, for one thing, might be confusing for her. But also, because it was Miss Emily—someone she was already fond of—he was worried that Lilly might get too attached. If things didn't pan out between him and her teacher, it would be one more thing the little girl had to lose.

It was tricky to keep Emily away, though, because frankly he was hooked on her. It would be terrifying, if it weren't such a mind-blowing high—though he supposed that's what all the addicts said. Dimitri couldn't stop thinking about her, couldn't stop texting her, and couldn't seem to lose the hard-on he'd been sporting since he'd first kissed her. After his years-long lack of physical touch, jobs and responsibilities seemed like excruciating obstacles. To keep somewhat sane, he'd been jerking off like a goddamn teenager, and scheming like a madman to get more time with Emily.

However, if he started lingering around Emily's rooms *every* day at lunchtime, hoping for another nooner—more people than Boggs were going to start talking. Dimitri didn't want to sabotage Emily's professional reputation just because he couldn't keep his dick in his pants. That wouldn't be fair. But…he also couldn't get another babysitter so soon after the last time—Lilly would almost certainly mutiny.

So, all that meant he needed to find a workaround. He wanted Emily like he wanted his next breath, but he couldn't have her in person at the moment. Dimitri was no genius, but he was pretty sure that left them with phone sex. Which he'd never done.

Seemed like the kind of thing he really didn't want to get wrong, either. Too filthy, and he ran the risk of sounding scary—too tame, and he'd likely end up feeling worse than before. Too bossy just sounded boring, but there was no way he was going to search the internet for help with that shit.

He was a grown man—he ought to be able to figure it out. Dimitri contemplated the idea off and on for most of the afternoon and evening.

He tabled the conundrum while he fed his kid, got her ready for bed, and read some stories with her. He kissed Lilly goodnight, turned on her nightlight, and shut her door. Dimitri went downstairs and turned on the television, but even the hockey season playoffs couldn't keep his interest.

Instead, he set the house alarm, shut off all the lights, and headed up to his room to think his problem through. When Emily called him at nine—like he'd known she would—Dimitri was sitting in the dark on the side of his bed, heart already beating fast. He had no idea how to ask for what he wanted, but he'd developed some ideas about how to proceed if she agreed. Unfortunately, if she thought he was weird or pervy, he expected there would be no recovering from that.

Somehow, though—in that capable way Emily had—she managed to lead right into it.

"What are you doing?" she asked him quietly.

Dimitri went with honesty, just to see where it took them. "Honestly? Sitting on my bed in the dark."

He could hear her soft laugh. "Me too," she said.

"Really?" Well, that was awfully helpful of her.

"Were you waiting for me?" Emily wondered.

He laughed darkly. "You have no idea."

"I might have a *little* idea," she teased.

Dimitri considered the situation. All signs seemed to be favorable, so he figured he might as well go for it. "I wish we were together right now," he told her, even though *wish* was an altogether inadequate word to describe what he was currently feeling.

"I do, too," Emily sighed, and the soft sound shot straight toward his groin. "What are you wearing?" she asked then. "I'm trying to picture you."

He gripped the back of his t-shirt and yanked it over his head, then stood and shucked off his sweats. In seconds, Dimitri was laying back against his pillows in only his boxers, his legs stretched out in front of him. Just in case.

"Not a whole lot," he smiled. He gave Emily a minute to digest that, then inquired, "And…you?"

Her silence was deafening and dragged on forever. At last, though, her voice slipped like silk along his ear. "Let's just say…the bare minimum."

Dimitri had to try a couple times to get his mouth to work right. "How bare a minimum are we talking?"

"The barest of the bare," she taunted.

He groaned. *Game on.* "Are you under the covers, Emily? Or spread out on top of your bed like a feast for me?"

He held his breath and could almost hear her smile through the phone line, "I'm on top."

"I want to touch your skin," he breathed, low and urgent. "Do it. Pet yourself for me."

"Where?" Her voice was breathless.

Dimitri forced his brain to come up with something. "Your stomach," he blurted out. "I love how soft your skin is there." It was true, but surely he could come up with something better— something sexier? He tacked on, "Now your breasts…cup them in your hands, and—"

Emily tried to stifle it, but he heard her moan. He was on the right track, for sure.

"—play with your nipples," he told her. He didn't think he'd ever spoken like that in bed before, but in the dark, with *her*, it wasn't nearly as difficult as he'd imagined. He heard rustling from her end of the line and had to readjust himself in his shorts.

"What are you doing?" Emily wanted to know. "Are you…are you touching yourself, too?"

"Do you want me to?" he rumbled.

"God, yes. *Please.*"

His heart was pounding in his chest. "How? Tell me."

"Uh, I don't know. I'm kind of…picturing your hand drifting down your chest toward your waistband."

"Now what?" He did as she instructed, then pushed his boxers off and out of the way. He didn't grip himself yet, though. As hard as he was, he still wanted to wait until she told him to.

She inhaled. "You first. Tell me what's next."

Dimitri swallowed. There was no way he was going to survive this, but his voice came out sounding strong and sure. "Stroke yourself, honey. Tell me if you're all slick and ready for me."

"I am *so* ready for you," she whimpered, and it was the most erotic thing he'd ever heard. "I don't think I can wait very long."

"Don't wait," he said. "Do it now. Get yourself there, Em, so I can hear you."

She was breathing fast. Dimitri longed to swallow those breaths in his mouth, to tangle his tongue with hers.

"You too," she gasped. "You do it, too. I can almost see you, Dimitri. Straddling my knees and stroking yourself…" Emily trailed off, but he thought they probably both had what they needed to finish things off.

He strained to listen for every little sound from her end that he could, but he couldn't hear much past the blood rushing in his ears and his heart hammering against his ribcage. He came embarrassingly fast and hard, in a rush against his stomach that shocked him with its heat. Dimitri mopped at himself with his cast-off shirt, but really only succeeded in spreading it around.

His cell was disconcertingly quiet against his ear, and he wondered if he'd lost her. "Emily?" he murmured. "You still there, honey?"

She hummed in her throat. "Oh God, yes. I can't believe we just did that."

He couldn't read her tone. "Me either," he admitted. "You okay?"

"More than okay, you big stud," she laughed. "I have to admit—I've never done that before. But…I think maybe I've been missing out."

"Ditto," he agreed. "Though I'd still rather do it in person."

"Agreed," Emily said. "And we will. Soon."

Unless she meant sometime in the next five minutes, it wouldn't be nearly soon enough. His breath was sawing in and out of his lungs. Dimitri's overheated skin was rapidly cooling, and without her body to physically nestle against him, he had no idea how to move forward. To save them from a painfully awkward silence, he told her the one truth that floated to the top of the stew swirling in his brain.

"I can't wait."

After barely any hesitation, Emily's voice piped up again, louder and more alert now, "Hey, can I ask you something strange?"

"Sure."

"Have you, like, been with many people?"

"Oh, legions," he replied drily. Why did that question make him feel ancient?

"Ah."

"Emily, I'm kidding. Why do you ask?"

"Because I…haven't. And after what we just did, I'm kind of wishing that weren't the case."

He blinked, trying to unravel her logic. Finally giving up, he capitulated, "I don't follow."

"Well…I liked it. A lot. And I'm afraid if there are other things that you want, I won't know enough to keep you…"

For some reason, her flash of uncertainty was impossibly endearing mere minutes after she'd seduced him into oblivion. "Keep me what?" Dimitri prodded.

She huffed out an embarrassed-sounding chuckle. "Just keep you, I guess."

He squeezed his eyes shut in disbelief. If anyone ought to be concerned about keeping someone interested, it was *him*.

"Sweetheart, believe me when I tell you, you have absolutely nothing to worry about on that score. I'm hardly some card-carrying Romeo, but you are definitely a goddess."

"Your flattery will get you everywhere," she said.

"God willing," he fired back.

"On that note," Emily said. "I should probably get going. I have a meeting with some parents before school tomorrow."

"I understand. Maybe I can stop by and say hello at lunch?"

"I hope you will."

"Then I will. Sleep tight, beautiful."

"Good night." And then she was gone.

Dimitri was abruptly conscious of the fact that he was sprawled naked and alone on his bed, his stomach sticky and his little daughter sleeping innocently just down the hall. He tossed his phone aside and leaped for the bathroom, then parked himself under the scalding spray of his shower until the water ran cold.

What did he think he was doing? He wasn't some twenty-year-old dude any longer, able to do whatever the hell he pleased. He was someone's father, someone's *only* parent. He couldn't plunge impulsively into a bacchanal with a younger woman just because he felt horny and deprived. He had to think this out.

He didn't even want to consider what Anna might have said about this. She'd probably have been appalled. He was acting like a creep.

Dimitri shuffled back to bed, but laid there for hours, torturing himself with all the ways he was failing at this impossible single-dad thing. Finally, aware that he was lurching headlong into martyr territory and desperate for some rest, he called up email on his phone. Searching through his contacts for Claudette's receptionist, he sent a request for an emergency appointment the next day. He needed to get some perspective before he screwed everything up. He had, after all, promised he'd try not to hurt her.

After a brief call first thing in the morning, Anna's mom graciously agreed to sit with Lilly, so Dimitri could sneak in an appointment with Claudette after work. His former mother-in-law had been excited enough to get the call, that he had to wonder if he'd been bringing Lilly to visit her grandparents often enough.

But that was a concern for another time. For now, Dimitri had to get through his current appointment. He'd struggled through a carefully-edited version of recent events, trying to communicate to his therapist why he was abruptly so off-kilter. His words, like his brain, seemed to be all over the map, though.

As she tended to do, Claudette accepted his mess of an explanation, and somehow magically transformed it into a series of logical statements that made perfect sense to him. She made Dimitri's decisions sound so normal, instead of like a dirty, depraved old man preying on a young innocent. She wasn't done, though.

"As to the guilt you mentioned," she said. "From what I understand, you and Anna loved each other very much. She was taken from you too soon, but perhaps try looking at it from her perspective. Real love is not miserly or punitive. I doubt very much that Anna would be comforted by you being lonely or miserable. My guess is that she would want you to be happy. To love and be loved."

"I hadn't thought about it that way," Dimitri murmured weakly. He'd been too busy beating himself up for his deficiencies.

"My second point would be this. Just like every person is different, so is every love. When it's wrong, no amount of wishful thinking or good intentions can force it into compliance. And when love is right, Dimitri, it doesn't always proceed in a measured, genteel way."

"It did with Anna."

"Well…Emily is not Anna, obviously. And I gotta tell you—the term 'love at first sight' exists for a reason. Sometimes people fall for each other like a ton of bricks, the second they lay eyes on each other."

Dimitri didn't seize up at the mention of the word love, like he might've only months earlier. But he didn't jump for joy, either. "How can I tell if it's love or infatuation, though? I'm hardly in a position to get that wrong right now."

"Your brain can only take you so far, Dimitri. At some point, you're going to have to listen to your gut and your heart, too," the doctor smiled.

Right—easier said than done.

AFTER TALKING HIS face off for close to an hour, Dimitri was reasonably clear on the notion that he wasn't feeling paralyzing guilt for "cheating" on Anna, so much as an equally-paralyzing terror that he was being irresponsible and rash for jumping feet-first into this thing with Emily.

It seemed a bit precipitous to be throwing around the "L" word so casually, but even he could acknowledge that the gut-level push-back he felt at the notion was more of a defense mechanism than a real resistance to the idea. And at least now he didn't feel like he was going to hell for being a normal adult man with normal adult needs.

Speaking of which, he'd taken the long way home, just so he could drive the road that ran along the side of the school property. Backing to that road was the building that housed the guest suites, and smack in the middle of the first floor were Emily's windows, with one dim light still on.

Now, Dimitri had to decide whether to call her again and risk a reprisal of last night's hot and heavy before he was quite ready for it. Or whether to wait another couple of days, to make *sure* he knew what he was doing.

He slowed down along the back side of campus, then turned the corner to pass the front gate. As if he'd conjured her with his thoughts alone, Emily left the tavern she'd gone to with him and crossed the street in front of his car, another man dogging her steps. She was too busy fielding the kisses of the handsy guy to even notice who was behind the wheel of the car—too busy leading her new acquisition toward her rooms.

Dimitri sat frozen in horror, witnessing the replica of his first night with Emily unfold before his eyes. Did she do that kind of thing all the time, despite what she'd told him? Was Dimitri an enormous dupe?

It took him a few minutes to realize Emily was laughing in scorn, not joy. As he watched, that scorn shifted to disbelief, then uncertainty. And then she wasn't laughing any longer—Emily looked worried. She was trying to fight the guy off.

Dimitri yanked the wheel to the side and pulled into a parking spot a few yards past the school gates. He was out of his seat and high-tailing it across the lawn a breath later, determined to get to Emily before that asshole could get her isolated and alone.

Chapter Eight

WHY *HAD* SHE agreed to meet Stuart tonight, anyway? Emily hadn't spoken to him in months, not since the enormous blow-up they'd had when she confronted him with proof of the wife he'd neglected to mention. She didn't even know how he'd figured out where she was.

But Stuart had sounded so calm and reasonable when he called and begged her to meet him at the tavern for a drink. He'd said he wanted to apologize for how things had ended between them, but that had been another lie. Emily had been feeling just cocky enough about how things were going with Dimitri, that she'd swallowed it easily.

Perhaps she had wanted to make Stuart pay for what he'd done to her—rub his nose in the fact that she'd moved on. But it had rapidly become clear that *sorry* was the last thing on her ex-boyfriend's mind. He was only in Annapolis on business and feeling frisky. Somehow, he'd thought she'd be interested.

She was such a fool to have fallen for his shit again. By the time Emily arrived, Stuart had already had a few, and was gunning for the kind of hook-up they'd shared before. This time, the only thing different was when Emily refused to play along.

She tried to leave. Emily abandoned her untouched glass of wine and marched out of the tavern with a head full of steam, intending to go straight home and punch a pillow or something for her idiocy. Stuart was acting stubborn, though, and followed her out.

When stubborn didn't work, he tried wheedling. That gave way to anger pretty quickly, though. And abruptly, Emily realized she'd done a very stupid thing when she led him onto the dark and lonely school grounds. Stuart wasn't taking no for an answer, and now there wasn't a soul around to stop him.

She picked up her pace and tried to double back toward the street, but her ex had oddly fast reflexes for someone who was sloppily drunk. His hand darted out and caught her upper arm—spinning Emily toward him so he could smash his mouth against hers.

Stuart's boozy kiss lasted only a second before he was wrenched away from her. Emily stumbled back, staggered to see *Dimitri* blocking her ex-boyfriend from getting to her. He'd appeared out of nowhere, but she wasn't going to waste time wondering how or why—she was just ridiculously grateful he had.

Dimitri bobbed and lunged on the dark lawn, parrying with drunk, married Stuart while her former flame attempted to get hold of Emily again. It was clear her current man wasn't buying Stuart's efforts to stake a claim on her. He wouldn't let Stu speak to her and wasn't taking too kindly to his attempts to catch Emily's eye, either.

Stuart was just enough of an asshole to be incensed at being thwarted. He pushed Dimitri back with two hands square on the taller man's chest. But all that did was give Dimitri enough room to drop Stuart like a bad habit.

The first strike darted out so fast, Emily found herself jumping back before her brain even registered what had happened—the heel of Dimitri's palm connecting with the underside of Stuart's chin with lethal precision. Stuart swayed, then lunged forward in an uncoordinated way. The next hit was nothing fancy, but extremely efficient—a solid line-drive punch to her ex-boyfriend's nose, which knocked him flat on his back.

Stuart groaned once, and then lay still—out cold on the grass. Emily gaped at him, then at Dimitri. Dimitri wasn't looking at her, though. He'd cocked his head and was studying the man he'd just laid out.

He inquired casually, "Is that guy's name Stu? Stu Facini?"

If Emily was surprised before, now she was completely gobsmacked. "How did you know that?"

"He screwed one of my partners in a land deal. Maybe ten years ago. He's a total dick."

Emily snorted—of *course*, he had. "Why am I not surprised?" she asked.

"Let me guess. He's the ex-boyfriend, isn't he?"

"I'm not proud of it," she sighed.

Dimitri smiled softly. "Come on," he gestured. "Let's get you out of here."

She dragged her heels, though, still impressed by how fast he'd neutralized the threat, so to speak.

"What did you *do* to him, anyway?" she breathed.

Dimitri was too quiet. Almost…sullen. "I'm sorry, it looked like he was hurting you," he explained flatly. He crossed his arms and looked out across the dark lawn, like he thought Emily was mad at him.

"He was," she assured him. She should have known how to take care of it, though, and was embarrassed that she hadn't. A light bulb clicked on in her brain, and Emily grabbed his sleeve. "Could you teach *me* how to do that?"

Dimitri's head snapped up, and his intense eyes locked on hers. Maybe that had been a tad too bloodthirsty but come *on*—a girl could never be too prepared.

Emily slipped her arm around his taut waist. "Please?"

Dimitri shook his head slightly, like he was dislodging something strange, then ran a hand through that dark silky hair of his.

"Uh, yeah. Sure," he said, seeming startled. "Of course. You ought to know how to fend off attackers, anyway. To be safe."

Emily looked back at Stuart again, the dark lump of him marring the otherwise pristine lawn. Dimitri took her arm gently and urged her away.

She went docilely but peered over her shoulder again after a few more paces. "Should we just leave him there like that? I'd hate for one of the kids to find him in the morning."

Dimitri glanced down at her. "You're right. Hang on—I'll call the security guard to come get him."

While he murmured quietly into his cell, the adrenaline of her encounter with Stuart started to wear off. Emily realized she really didn't want to be in her empty apartment alone that night. She was more shaken than she wanted to admit by the way her too-slick ex had edged far into the realm of frightening.

When he disconnected his call, Dimitri took one look at her face, and seemed to understand.

"Hey, are you okay?"

"Not totally," Emily confessed. "I'm still not sure what that was. Stuart…said he wanted to explain what happened with us. Before."

Dimitri's nose wrinkled, but he resisted saying whatever snarky comment had occurred to him.

Emily said, "I don't know why I met him. I think maybe I wanted to gloat a little, but then he was getting gross and handsy, and he followed me over here…and you showed up at the perfect moment." She studied him in the dim light from the lampposts lining the brick walkway. "What were you doing here, anyway?"

Dimitri rubbed at his chin. "I had to run out for an appointment earlier, so Anna's mom came by to watch Lilly for me. I was on my way home when you two literally crossed the street right in front of my car."

It seemed like an impossible coincidence, but what did she know? Emily had no idea where Dimitri and Lilly lived.

"Well, I am very glad you did."

"Listen, maybe you shouldn't be alone tonight. Do you want to, uh…" There was an infinitesimal pause before he continued.

"…come by my place? I'll get rid of Grandma, and if we're quiet, Lilly won't ever have to know you were there."

His discomfort eased when she said, "If you're sure it's okay, I would really appreciate that. I could follow you there—that way I can duck out in the morning before Lilly wakes up. Then you won't have to explain anything to her."

"You don't mind being sneaky?"

"Of course not. I totally understand."

"Thank you," he said. "I'm parked right over there but I only live about three blocks from here. It's up to you whether you want to ride with me or follow me home."

Follow him home—it sounded too much like something a wayward puppy might do, but Emily wasn't really in a position to be nit-picky. That didn't mean she had to set herself up for a walk of shame in the morning, though.

"If you'll walk me to my car, I'll drive myself," she told him.

Dimitri nodded and took her hand, led Emily to the back lot where her car was stashed, then hopped in so she could drive him to his.

She trailed his sedan through the dark and quiet streets. As he'd indicated, three blocks later, he pulled into the driveway of a large brick townhouse in an upscale cul-de-sac. Emily cut her headlights and waited behind the wheel, while Dimitri ducked in the front door.

Moments later, he escorted an older blonde out to her Mercedes and stood in the driveway watching her roll away. Did he hesitate a moment too long before turning and beckoning to Emily? She was probably reading too much into it—Dimitri's smile was plenty warm when he met her at the foot of his front stairs. He leaned down to press a lingering kiss to her lips, then brought Emily inside.

She stood silently in the entryway while he reset the house alarm, then crept after him when he took her hand and pulled her deeper into the house. Down a hallway, through a family room lit only by the tiny blue lights blinking from his entertainment unit, to a set of stairs rising at the side of the room. Dimitri paused to listen, holding a finger up to his lips.

Maybe Emily was in shock, but the covert routine suddenly seemed hilariously overdone. She grinned and motioned Dimitri closer.

"Look at you." she giggled into his ear. "You're like some kind of sex ninja."

He grinned right back at her, whispering, "Pipe down and tiptoe. I'll lift you over the squeaky stair when we get to it."

Every step, and every breath seemingly glaringly loud when they edged past Lilly's closed bedroom door, but finally they were shut inside Dimitri's very masculine bedroom, with its dark-painted walls and simple gray bedding. Emily looked around. This was no twenty-something's crash pad. A real adult man lived here, and it was impossibly arousing.

She spun around to say something to him, but Dimitri was already there, pulling her close and tangling his tongue with hers. He'd been her guardian angel tonight, and now he'd upped the ante by inviting her to his home. Emily knew they had to be quiet but being in his space was incredible feeling. If it weren't for his lips locked onto hers, she might not be able to keep the sounds in.

She tugged him toward that big mahogany bed of his, but when her legs hit the mattress, the headboard knocked against the wall. It was a short sound, but it was loud. Dimitri's head jerked up with a frown, and she saw him begin to lose focus.

So, Emily edged around the side of the bed and began unbuttoning her blouse. As she'd hoped, Dimitri kicked off his shoes and shucked off his long-sleeved shirt, and those large, hot hands of his were suddenly *everywhere*.

"God. I want you so much. I can't believe you're *here*. I want you here," he told her, low and urgent.

Emily shrugged out of her shirt and bra and perched on the edge of the bed. "Right here?"

He unbuttoned his shorts and dropped them to the floor, giving her an excellent view of what she hoped was coming her way.

"Almost," he said.

Which was probably how she ended up bent over the bed getting the daylights loved out of her—with a corner of his pillow clamped between her teeth so her moans wouldn't wake his kid. If someone had told Emily two years ago that it would be the most stupefying, brain-melting sex of her life, she never would've believed them.

Laying snuggled against his side afterward, she basked in the way Dimitri played with tendrils of her hair.

"Your hair is so pretty," he told her. "You're like a fairy princess with all this stuff."

"Now you sound like Lilly."

"No, I'm serious. I would never have guessed that it wasn't your real color."

Well, that was strange. "What are you talking about? It is."

"But—"

Emily scowled. "But, *what?*"

Dimitri blushed a vivid crimson, stammering, "I just thought…since your hair is so dark *other* places, that—"

She cut him off. "That is a total myth, you big doofus."

"Well how am I supposed to know that? I have all brothers!" he protested.

"So, what! It's not like you've never dated. *And* you were married for *how* many years? What color was Anna's hair?"

"Suddenly I am not comfortable with the direction this is going."

"Oh please. Was she a blonde, or not?"

"Yes. She was," he relented. "But she dyed it religiously every six weeks, so I doubt she was an authority on this particular topic."

"Okay, look," Emily explained. "A different set of genes regulates each area of body hair—I did a report on it in high school Biology. It's why so many Irish guys have red beards, no matter what color hair they have on their head. And it's why it is entirely possible for a woman to have one color hair up top and another color down south."

Dimitri looked fascinated. "*Huh*," he said.

"Ever since I was a kid, I've had light hair on my head, but dark eyebrows and lashes—and, clearly, dark hair elsewhere. You catch my drift?"

"I…think so. And that's nuts. You would not believe how many dudes dwell on that little bit of misinformation."

"I'm not surprised," she snorted. "But, I am a bit shocked I had something new to teach *you*."

"Why? I could've predicted that."

"I don't know—aforementioned life experience, I guess. So…you're not…I don't know—put-off or anything, are you?"

"Are you kidding?" Dimitri tucked his arms across his chest defensively. "You are how you are. And I don't recall saying I didn't like it."

"That's true," Emily mused. "You liked me plenty about fifteen minutes ago."

Dimitri reached for her and pulled her close again, murmuring, "Oh, trust me, I did." His kisses gradually grew longer and deeper, and Emily worried they were headed for horizontal boogie territory again.

"I should go," she whispered in the dark.

His arms held her tight. "Not yet. Please."

"I don't want to stay too long," Emily worried.

"We still have time," he reassured her, and bent to her neck.

DIMITRI WAS HELLBENT on maximizing the time they had together—worshiping Emily's skin long into the wee hours. And, despite her good intentions, it felt too good to lay next to him— tucked warm and safe against his side where ugly pasts couldn't touch them—to leave when she should have.

At some point, they must have fallen asleep, even though Emily hadn't meant to stay. Dimitri was already up and gone when she awoke. He'd left her a t-shirt and some gym shorts to wear, all too long for her. Taking the cue, she got dressed in his clothes, then sat on the edge of his bed to think.

On the chair in the corner of his room, her clothes from the night before were folded in a neat pile next to her purse and jacket. She wandered over and fished her phone out of her bag to check the screen. There was a missed call from Stuart, but instead of listening to the message, Emily blocked the number like she should have months ago.

She was kicking herself for oversleeping and couldn't decide if she should hide up there until she could slip out unnoticed or attempt to leave right then. Lilly might already know she was there, and perhaps they were waiting downstairs for her to make an appearance—Emily could smell coffee and food aromas wafting up from the kitchen.

At last, she stepped quietly down the stairs, still trying to figure out how to play it. Halfway down, she heard Lilly ask her father, "Is Miss Emily going to be my new Mommy now?" Emily froze.

"No, of course not," his low voice rumbled. "No one could ever replace your mom, Peach. You know that."

Well, that hurt. Even though they'd only been dating a handful of weeks, Emily had thought she and Dimitri had a connection—that he was ready to open himself up to something bigger when the time came.

But of course, that was her current M.O., wasn't it? Always falling too fast or too hard for the wrong man. If Dimitri knew Emily had no long-term potential so soon, then her infatuation with him was obviously very one-sided.

Lilly spotted her before Emily could make a break for it and dash back upstairs.

"Miss Emily, look! We have apple juice!" she called from her stool at the kitchen island.

Emily hesitated on the threshold, then squared her shoulders and stepped into the room.

"What!" She feigned amazement for Lilly's sake. "That's great!" Emily pulled out a chair at their little round table and perched on the seat. Dimitri was cooking something in a pan on the stove, but he didn't look up at her. Didn't even wink or smile.

Between the time they'd fallen asleep and now, something had obviously gone wrong, and Emily didn't have to be a genius to figure out what *that* was. She was only supposed to be an occasional roll in the hay, nothing more—and she'd overstayed her welcome.

She must have been making even better progress with Lilly on the reading front than she'd thought, too, because with only a cursory glance that cute little girl read Emily's expression like it spelled "C is for Cat."

"You can't be our new Mommy," Lilly pointed out forlornly. "Daddy said."

Dimitri banged the pan, and Emily swallowed past the lump in her throat. Well, there it was. Trust a five-year-old to state the obvious.

To buy time, she confirmed, "You asked him that?"

Lilly's eyes were big and sad when she nodded. Then, she swiveled around on her stool to check on her father's progress with her breakfast, effectively giving Emily the cold shoulder.

Emily stood up so fast, she banged her knee on the table leg, and made the entire piece of furniture squeak across the tile floor.

"I wish I could stay for breakfast," she announced loudly. "But I need to head out." She felt like an idiot for dressing in Dimitri's clothes instead of her own, so she trotted upstairs to rectify that misstep.

In moments, she was armored in her own outfit again and scooping her purse onto her shoulder in the foyer. She caught Lilly's eye in the kitchen and gave her a jaunty wave, like this whole disaster was No Big Deal.

"I'll see you on Tuesday, Lilly," she called. Then, after only a second of debate, she tacked on, "Bye, Dad." He'd yet to speak a word.

The little girl started shoveling scrambled eggs into her mouth. Instead of replying, she lifted her small stuffed duck in salute.

Dimitri came around the island wiping his hands on his shorts. When he finally looked Emily in the face, his eyes were shadowed—tortured.

"Let me walk you out," he murmured.

Emily backed away, darting a glance back at his kid. "That's not necessary."

Dimitri's eyes shot up and he frowned, "Yes, it is."

Chapter Nine

DIMITRI SLID PAST Emily's stiff body to open the front door, followed her out, then pulled the wood panels mostly shut behind him. Based on Emily's stormy expression, his kid didn't need to hear whatever happened next.

An unwieldy knot was in his throat, blocking his air, and he tried to dislodge it. "When you get home," he said finally, "Have campus security walk you to your place. Joe left me a message last night that Stu was gone when they went to look for him. Hopefully, he didn't find his way inside your apartment somehow, but better to be safe than sorry."

"That's it?" Emily yelped. "*That's* what you wanted to tell me so badly?"

It wasn't, but it *was* important. "Yeah." Dimitri shrugged. "Text me later, so I know you got home safe."

The sound she made was dismissive and then some.

"Listen…I'm sorry," he told her. "I didn't mean for it to go like this."

Emily shook her head and kept her distance, even though they were out of sight of Lilly. "No worries," she managed sullenly.

One peek at her face and he sighed again, "Come on, you know how kids are. They always ask the thing you're least prepared for, at the worst possible moment." Which was true. Mostly.

But she fired back, "It sounded like you had a ready answer, though."

Dimitri folded his arms tightly across his chest. It seemed impossible to believe that those same arms had held Emily within them only hours before—now they were rather efficiently keeping her out, weren't they?

"It just came out," Dimitri explained. "It wasn't intended to hurt you."

Emily refocused on him. "Even so, I think I know my marching orders now."

Oh, she was pissed, all right. "Don't be like that," he frowned.

"It's not like I thought we were going to ride off into the sunset after such a short time together," she retorted. "But I did think we had a…connection."

"We do." It was a knee-jerk response—one meant to placate, not convince. Even Dimitri could hear it.

"You sure about that?" Emily inquired. Her smile sat bitterly on her lips.

Her tone left him unaccountably miffed. "What's that supposed to mean?"

Honestly, what did Emily want from him? He couldn't control what came out of Lilly's mouth, any more than he'd been able to keep them from oversleeping this morning.

"I guess I thought you were maybe a bit more over your wife than you actually are," she explained. "More fool I." She turned away.

If Emily thought she could exit stage left after dropping that nasty zinger, she was sadly mistaken. Dimitri felt his scowl deepen, and he shifted back.

"I mean…It's not like you just flip a switch or something, Em."

"I'm aware, *Dee*," Emily said testily.

He flinched. What, now nicknames weren't allowed?

"But I'm also not into being your rebound fling," she said. "Sorry."

She didn't sound sorry—she sounded disgusted. Dimitri couldn't come up with anything to say about that little gem. He simply stood there like a dope on his stoop, gripping his doorknob while Emily took the six steps to her car, got in, and drove away.

How did people actually manage stuff like this? Dimitri knew he'd blown it big-time but didn't have a clue what he ought to have said differently. He felt like a fool, impossibly ill-equipped to interact with other humans—and *that* could get very, very lonely.

BACK IN THE kitchen, Lilly was working on an Olympic-caliber pout, and had fat, lazy tears rolling down her cheeks. She gripped her stuffed duck under her chin and was examining something in her pale, pudgy little hand. When Dimitri walked in, she jumped and slipped whatever it was into the pocket of her pajamas.

He tensed, immediately suspicious. It wasn't like Lilly to hide things from him.

"What do you have there?" he wondered.

If it was possible to look both sweet and innocent *and* guilty as sin—then that was his kid.

"Nothing," she chirped. And…now Lilly was lying to his face.

Dimitri shook his head and pulled out the stool next to hers to lean on, so he wouldn't loom quite so much over her. He held out his palm. "Come on. Let's see it."

Lilly blinked up into his face for a full minute before she finally relented. The duck crept higher, covering her quivering lip, and she handed over her contraband.

When Dimitri saw what it was, his blood ran cold.

"Where did you get this?" he demanded. Anna's gold necklace, with its small round Athena pendant—he'd gotten it for her in Athens at the start of their honeymoon.

"In there." Lilly pointed toward the living room. "Mommy told me where it was."

The necklace had been in a small wooden box, also from Greece, up on the mantel. Little Lilly could never have reached it on her own.

"But how did you climb so high?"

Lilly shrugged, and the tears pooling in her wide eyes spilled over again. While he watched them, it dawned on Dimitri what she'd just said.

"Lills, did you say that *Mommy* told you where it was?"

"Mm-hm." His poor kid was clearly trying to figure out if she was in trouble or not, so Dimitri did his best to school his expression into something calm. But his mind was reeling.

"When did she do that? Do you remember?"

"Yes, Daddy," she said, and her tone underlined the *Duh* she meant. "It was only last night."

What the hell? "Did you, uh…was Mommy *here*? Did you see her?"

Lilly nodded. "We talked about stuff. But I was sleeping."

"I see."

So…if he had it straight, his dead wife had chosen last night—of all possible nights—to visit their daughter and have a conversation. And Dimitri had missed it, because he'd been too busy getting laid by Anna's replacement. *Lovely.*

Lilly must have been unperturbed by whatever his face was registering, because she chattered on, "Mommy said I was uh-posed to give her necklace to Miss Emily, so she would be strong like Mommy and love us best. But then you said *no* and Miss Emily left. That was very bad, Daddy."

Dimitri stared in shock at his baby girl, betrayal writ large across her small, perfect face. Her dark curls tumbled haphazardly around her head, and that duck of hers was tucked under her chin again so Lilly could chew him out unimpeded.

"Lilly…is *that* why you asked if Miss Emily could be your new Mommy?" He'd assumed it was because his daughter had somehow seen him in bed with Emily and jumped to the natural conclusion of a five-year-old. Trust *his* life to be far weirder than that.

She nodded. "Daddy, I think you made Miss Emily sad."

He had. He'd known it, but at the time had seen no other way out.

"Mommy is going to yell at you," his kid added, matter-of-factly.

Dimitri dearly hoped not. It would be a seriously awful capstone to what was already shaping up to be a lousy day. He could only imagine what his therapist would say when he told her that Lilly was now apparently talking to ghosts—benevolent ghosts, but still. Dimitri could surely expect an "out of the mouths of babes" comment. And he could probably also count on Claudette coming up with something along the lines of "what a wonderful gift, to receive Anna's imprimatur through Lilly."

He sighed and ruffled Lilly's hair. "Well, Peach—maybe if you see her again, you can put in a good word for me. But, now I think we need to get ready for school."

AFTER HE DROPPED Lilly off, his mind circled back to Emily's final words to him. Rebound? Dimitri wasn't using Emily as a *rebound*, was he? Maybe he hadn't actually been on any dates since Anna had died—and hadn't even been interested. But that didn't mean he was a selfish bastard putting the moves on his kid's teacher, just so he could bag her and tag her—so to speak.

Abruptly, Dimitri thought about the first couple nights he'd left Lilly with her grandparents, so he could go out with friends, after…well, *after*. A few dudes from the company had allowed him about eight months to wallow before bullying him into some happy hours. Sitting in those dark, loud bars had been utter torture.

After years of domesticity, with an elegant, sophisticated woman in his bed at night and Lilly sleeping peacefully in her crib down the hall…Dimitri had hated every moment of the mating dance swirling around him. He'd despised that line of middle-aged men at the bar, pretending to watch sports on the TVs while surreptitiously checking out the bartenders and cocktail waitresses. He'd been repulsed by the venal women all dressed to the nines, primed like birds of prey as they tossed their hair and assessed net worth—oh, and looked for love, of course.

Dimitri had been about as capable of love back then as a fountain pen. His ability to feel that emotion had gone cold along with his wife—and dragging him an hour away from his new home to rub his nose in that fact, Friday after Friday, hadn't exactly been sporting. Dimitri had stopped going, but it had taken months longer before his old coworkers had stopped asking him along.

He'd once landed the love of a good woman, and they'd made a baby girl as soft and pretty as a tiny ripe peach, but life had seen fit to rob him of half that good fortune. Dimitri hadn't understood why then, and likely never would. He'd simply become a robot parading around in human skin, because for a long time, that was the only way to keep going. He'd retained only enough humanity to be a good father to Lilly.

Something had changed, though. Dimitri had to wonder what was different about Emily Tucker—what it was about her that had his blood singing and feelings jerking back online like a thief had hotwired his entire emotional substation. If such a thing were even possible, Emily was certainly capable of it.

It wasn't just that she'd never known him as "Anna's husband," hadn't know Dimitri as one half of a pair, in a social circle that continued to exist despite missing a critical piece of itself. It wasn't only that the relentless passage of time—of *years*—had smoothed out the jagged edges of his tragedy second by tortuous second.

It was that Emily and her big blue eyes seemed to see *him*. *All* of him, not only the one part that she should be acquainted with—the part that was Lilly's dad. Emily looked at Dimitri like a man who could—and would—protect her. A man who enjoyed experiencing the world around him, with her at his side. A reader, a martial artist, a cook, and a lover. A man who, after too long in the dark, suddenly felt everything in the light a little too keenly.

For the first time in too long, Dimitri was a whole person, and that was all thanks to Emily. He'd begun living his life again, making plans for a future beyond the stale existence he'd decelerated into. That wasn't the work of some unimportant rebound.

That was magic, and Dimitri knew in his soul that no other woman could've pulled it off. Only Emily, with her wide-open heart and guileless affection could've disarmed him enough to scale his fortress walls. It would take Dimitri decades to repay that kind of gift, and that was…okay, actually.

He had to see her—to tell her what she'd done. But when Dimitri did, he wanted to be able to offer her something back. Something to show her he was serious about her, and them. Something Emily could hold onto, besides his and Lilly's hands.

ANNA'S MOM CALLED him that afternoon. When Dimitri picked up, she seemed flustered—maybe because she'd been hoping to get his voice mail. And after the way he'd frog-marched her out of the house last night, Dimitri wasn't positive he'd want to talk to him, either.

"Hello?"

"Oh! Hi, it's Marcie." Dimitri was immediately put on guard by her nervous voice.

Why would Anna's mother be calling, unless she'd left something behind? "What can I do for you, Marcie?"

"Is this a bad time?"

He'd already fixed the broken locker doors on the first floor and couldn't get in to replace the English teacher's burned-out ceiling bulbs until her fourth period let out. It was as good a time as any, and Dimitri told her so.

"I didn't want to keep you from your guest last night, but I thought I'd call today to let you know…" Marcie paused a long moment before powering on, "You don't have to hide that you're dating again from Phil and me. We understand why you might not want to tell Lilly right away, but we're all adults. We realize that your life isn't over and that you need…companionship. For heaven's sake, it's been three years, Dimitri. No one in their right mind could accuse you of not mourning Anna properly. And I just…you didn't have to pretend that you had therapy." She broke off to catch her breath. "Unless you're dating your doctor? I'd strongly advise against *that*."

Dimitri tried to catch up to her flurry of words. "No, I…I did have an appointment."

"That may be, but you also had a date." Marcie left no room for argument.

"But if you knew she was there, why didn't you say anything?" he wondered.

"It seemed crass to point it out at the time, when you were both taking such pains to be discreet. I didn't want to embarrass you then, and it's not my intention to embarrass you now."

"She's just a friend," Dimitri explained. "She ran into a little trouble with her ex, and I was able to help her out on my way home, that's all." Which was kind of true.

"I'm sure she's very nice," Marcie soothed. "And son, we both know that you'd never do anything to jeopardize Lilly's well-being. Don't worry about that. We simply wanted to reassure you that we are really okay with you looking after *yourself*, in addition to our granddaughter."

"Marcie, I…" Dimitri inhaled a deep, settling breath. "Thank you. You and Phil have always been very kind to me. To us."

"You took good care of Anna when she was suffering. Phil and I are too practical to expect you to suffer needlessly now, too. Anna wouldn't have wanted that for you or Lilly, and neither do we."

"That's very generous of you."

"We prefer to think of it as human. Now—I know you're at work. You should go. Just be sure to call us if you end up needing a sitter again, okay?"

"Of course, I will. Thanks again."

"Don't mention it."

His circle of acquaintances was lining up to sign off on the new relationship, it seemed. Dimitri didn't even need to guess what his own parents might say. They had been joined at the hip for most of their lives and had been heart-broken for him when his wife had died. If Dimitri found a new woman to love, they would trip all over themselves to ease his way.

Again, Dimitri's brain circled back to those guys who'd tried unsuccessfully to pull him into the light. While their methods left something to be desired, their intentions had been good. At least two were still at his old company and might be able to help him get his fledgling idea off the ground. And the more he considered all the angles, the better that sounded. It had to work, too—Emily was too rare and special for him to lose her now.

Chapter Ten

I T HAD TAKEN some convoluted maneuvering, but for days Emily had managed to avoid Dimitri like the plague. And now that she had, she thought she was back to looking and acting like a reasonable facsimile of a functional adult, too.

That assumption went out the window when the school's headmistress made an appearance in her classroom, though. Not surprisingly, it was smack in the middle of Lilly's regular morning session.

"Hey, Dr. Thompson," Emily greeted her. "What can I do for you?"

"Oh, just making the rounds," the woman replied airily. She wandered over to watch Lilly working on her puzzle, then drifted to the opposite corner of the room.

When Emily followed, Cecily turned to her with a small smile. "On some days, Lilly looks so much like her mother," she said.

"You knew her?" Emily hadn't realized the other woman had that close of a connection to the Tsiros family, though she supposed she should have. The headmistress had hired Dimitri at the suggestion of her sister—his therapist—after his wife had passed.

"Who, Anna?"

Emily nodded. "I saw some pictures, but it's hard to tell from those what she was like."

"Oh, she was something. Smart. Sophisticated. Very elegant and refined, but she wasn't cold. You know, she seemed like she could still have fun." The doctor picked at some invisible lint on her sleeve. "I gather she was quite the society darling before she fell ill."

Emily peered over at Lilly, frowning down in concentration exactly like her dad would. She only saw Dimitri all over the little girl's face, but maybe that was simply because she'd never known Anna.

"It's hard to picture him with someone like that," she told Cecily.

"Maybe now. Dimitri was different when they first came here, though. They were quite an indomitable pair, but a sickness like she had…" The woman shook her head. "It changes people."

"I imagine so."

"For Anna, it made an already-strong woman tougher, even though it was physically devastating. I'm sure she must have shown her husband a more vulnerable face, but we certainly never saw it."

Emily was almost afraid to ask, though she suspected it was why Cecily had decided to come by. "What about Dimitri?"

The headmistress shook her head again, thinking. "I don't know how to describe it. It was as if the bricks of his house were razed to the ground one day, then rebuilt into a completely new and different structure with the same face. Still a house. Still solid. Just…not the same one that stood there before."

"Hmm," Emily murmured, trying to wrap her head around the kind of grief and fear and fury that could remold a person like that.

Cecily took a deep breath and refocused on Emily. "Which is kind of the point I wanted to make to you. Dimitri and Anna might have been a terrific match when they married each other, but he's a gentler man now. He's more open to other viewpoints and perspectives, and…kinder in general, I suppose. Maybe he's realized that life is just too short to not appreciate the gifts you've been given."

Emily turned toward the little girl. "You mean like Lilly."

"Clearly. But I also mean his second chance at love."

Emily froze, realizing at last what the whole conversation had been about. Much like the entire school staff had probably noticed her and Dimitri spending time together, everyone had plainly also noticed that there now was trouble in paradise. While that wasn't totally unexpected, what the headmistress had just said *was*.

Across the room, the little girl finished fitting her puzzle pieces together, each of the letter shapes finally connecting to form the sentence she wanted. She looked up at them with a victorious grin.

"Look!" Lilly called, pointing at the table.

"Marvelous," Dr. Thompson told her with a smile.

Then Cecily squeezed Emily's shoulder. "Just think about it," she encouraged. "Father and daughter are both very special people."

"I will," Emily agreed. "Thank you."

It was a remarkably kind gesture, she had to admit—even if Emily suspected she'd have little say in what Dimitri ultimately decided to do.

"And Emily?" Cecily added. "Don't forget you're special, too."

Lilly had scampered over to tug on her hand. "Right!" the little girl agreed. She waved cheerily to the headmistress, then led Emily back to her table to show her what she'd accomplished.

She'd used her interlocking wood letters to spell out *Lilly lovs Dady Miss Emly an kats*.

Emily grinned, warming from the inside out. Special, indeed.

"That is pretty amazing," she announced. "Now let me show you how we can make it even better."

EMILY WAS READING with Ben again, congratulating herself on the samurai book that had finally grabbed his interest, when the boy's attention was caught by something dark moving across the lawn outside. Shifting to the side so she could peer out the window, she realized after a moment that it was a *who* they were looking at, not a *what*.

It was Dimitri, approaching across the grass in long, loping strides—cleaned-up and sharp as a tack in an exquisite, dark three-piece suit. Where had he been? Why would he be dressed like that?

Ben scowled and echoed her thoughts, "Why does Mr. Tsiros look like that?"

"I have no idea," Emily told him. "He looks very fancy, doesn't he?"

"He looks weird," the kid replied.

"You don't like it?" she asked, watching Dimitri loom closer. Emily did—she liked it a *lot*. After seeing him in mostly an assortment of handyman coveralls and gym clothes for weeks, she never would've guessed he could dress up quite like that. Too bad he'd made it eminently clear they had no future together.

Ben just shook his head, looking confused. He propped his book back up from where he'd dropped it in his lap and cleared his throat. "Ready?" he asked, pulling Emily's attention back to him.

"Yup," she agreed. She glanced outside one last time as Dimitri veered off the path toward Cecily's office. "Go for it," she urged.

Dimitri didn't want her. And therefore, Emily was not allowed to want him. So, she wouldn't—it was as simple as that.

WHEN EMILY WALKED Ben to the door thirty minutes later, Dimitri was waiting for her—leaning against the brick wall of the building like it was the most normal thing in the world. He greeted Ben with a gentle smile in complete opposition to the power suit, then watched the boy trot away.

At last, he turned to Emily. His eyes were soft and searching.

"Hey. How have you been?" he asked her.

She hated to admit that his dismissal had affected her in the least, but still found herself blurting out, "I've been better." Maybe it was the concern written all over his face. Or…maybe it was the basic desire to make sure he knew he'd hurt her.

Dimitri's eyebrows pinched together, and he looked regretful.

"I'm really sorry about the other morning," he said. "And I have things I'd love to tell you. But…if this is a bad time, I could—"

"No!" Emily interjected, before he could talk himself out of whatever he'd come there for. "This is, uh…this is a fine time." Abruptly, her parting words to him days ago filtered through her brain in a different light, and she realized she might have been a tad…harsh.

Dimitri indicated a park bench situated a few feet away, on the path that wound through the campus. "Do you want to sit?"

"Okay."

Dimitri leaned back and made himself comfortable, draping his arm across the back of the bench. Emily pulled her knee up and sat sideways, so she wouldn't be tempted to crawl into the shelter of his arms and could stare down at the buttons of his jacket. That way, she didn't have to look into those melting chocolate pools he called eyes.

She'd thought she was doing fine. But now, faced with Dimitri in the flesh, she realized that it had been a lie. Emily was sad and hurt and disappointed that he'd decided she couldn't fill his first wife's shoes, before ever really giving her a chance. She was furious that she got no say, but mostly she just missed him. Dimitri was an irresistible mix of tenderness and passion that she hadn't known existed before meeting him. Before…falling for him.

To keep from thinking about that, she asked, "Is this your suit?"

He touched her shoulder lightly with his fingertips. "Who else would it belong to? Of course, it's mine." Then he peered at her face. "Why?"

"It fits you beautifully," she confessed.

"I used to think so, too. Not so much anymore, though."

Emily raised her gaze from the subtle sheen of his blue silk tie to ask, "What do you mean?"

"Well…it's very corporate. And I just don't see myself getting back to that place anytime soon. Maybe someday, but not now. Lilly is too young, and to be honest, it probably wouldn't be good for me, either."

"So, why are you wearing it? I think you freaked Ben out a little bit."

"I had a meeting," he said. "Wait, let me start over. I've had an idea knocking around in my head for a while now, but I realized this week that it was time to stop treading water and actually swim toward the goal." Dimitri brushed his knuckles lightly across her cheek. "Two goals, actually. Did I mention that I'm sorry?"

"You did," Emily confirmed. "You're being sort of cryptic, though. Might you be more forthcoming?"

Dimitri's eyes lost some of their wariness as he gazed at her. "I might. I also…might have purchased a building today that I've had my eye on. It used to be a tile showroom, I think. But once I fix it up…" he trailed off and looked away, like he was seeing a picture in his mind of what he wanted to do.

"What?" Emily prompted him.

He unbuttoned his collar button, loosened his tie a little, then refocused on her. "I thought it would make a good *tae kwon do* studio. I thought I could give lessons. Maybe teach some classes."

"By yourself?" The thought of Dimitri getting in over his head worried her.

"Actually, no. I reached out to some folks I used to know when I was still competing, and a few of them said they'd be able to pick up some classes, too."

He had the smallest smile on his face, but he looked so happy—like he was lit up from the inside out. He'd make a terrific instructor, too. Between the way he helped Ben and the way he'd taught Emily some of the basics of self-defense here and there, Dimitri was a natural teacher. Exactly like he was with Lilly.

Emily smiled back at him, feeling lighter than she had in days. When she had an "idea knocking around" in her brain, it almost never emerged looking as polished as this. Dimitri had worked on this one—made it shine for her.

"All you need now is a business plan," she joked.

But instead of laughing, Dimitri pulled back a little to extract a thick envelope from inside his suit jacket.

"Right here," he said. "I couldn't exactly go to the meeting without it. Want to see?"

"Maybe later."

Like a magician doing a card trick, he fanned the papers in his hand to show her a second envelope behind the first.

Emily frowned and pointed. "What's that one?"

"I might've also purchased a new house."

"*Might've?*"

He nodded eagerly. "Uh-huh."

"To live in?"

"That's the plan." His grin grew wider.

"Where is it?" she asked suspiciously. If this whole production was so he could come say *goodbye* to her...

"Not too far from here. It's not huge, but it's right on the Severn river, and the kitchen has been totally remodeled."

"Dimitri—that must have cost you a small fortune," Emily said.

"Well...yes and no. The guy who sold me the other building is retiring and moving to Florida. When he heard I have a daughter, he made a little joke about making it a package deal. That had a good ring to it, so...we ran by and took a look. Long story short, I ended up making him an offer." Dimitri shrugged, like that kind of thing happened to people every day.

Emily marveled, "Boy, when you decide to stop *treading water*, you really don't mess around."

"That's true," he acknowledged. "It's sort of why I'm here."

"Oooookay," she drawled.

"Why don't you come see the house."

"Right now?"

"Yeah. I'll go get Lilly. We can all go together."

"Now."

He nodded. "Yes."

"Why?" Emily asked.

"Why not?"

"Because, it doesn't matter what I think?"

"I disagree. If you don't like it, you might not want to spend any time there with us."

"Is that what you want? Me…spending time with you and Lilly?"

"Yes, Emily, that is exactly what I want. I want to spend a lot of time with just you and me, and also a lot of time with you and me and Lilly. I want to get to know you better, and I want to treat you right, and I want to look forward to the future again. A future that has you smack in the middle of it."

"You're just saying that because of the rebound crack I made," she muttered guiltily. "By the way, I was totally out of line with that. I'm sorry."

"It's okay. I understand why you said it. But I need you to know that I don't feel that way about you, okay?"

"Okay, but—what do *I* have to offer you guys?"

"What do you mean?"

"I'm not sure what I can contribute, you know? I mean, I'm a total novice here. You're already a parent, and a bit older than me—"

Dimitri protested, "It's not like I'm Father Time over here!"

"I get that," Emily said. "But you *have* lived more years than me. You've been married. You're a parent. You simply have more life experience than I do. I don't want you guys to feel like I'm dead weight, never knowing what to do."

"Emily…" Dimitri hesitated. "I don't see it that way. I've had a different life than you, that's true. But just because it was different, doesn't automatically make it better. You've probably done a ton of things I haven't, just by being a woman. Just by being *you*. We have different families, and personalities, and educations, and I bet you know a *lot* of things I don't. You knew about the hair genes," he smirked, poking her in the arm.

Emily rolled her eyes. "Okay, that's hardly a critical body of knowledge. But tell me this—what about Anna? You and Lilly both loved her so much. How could I ever hope to compete with that?"

He had an answer ready for that question, too. "Luckily it's not a competition. Yes, we loved her and always will. Yes, she will always have a role in our lives, simply because she was my wife and Lilly's mom. But that doesn't mean there isn't room for you, too. If you wanted it, you could have an equally important place in our hearts."

Dimitri leaned toward her and tilted his head to rest against hers, then slipped an arm around Emily's shoulders. "It's not one or the other, you know? It's sort of…both. Like Anna started the relay with us, then passed the baton to you to continue the race. If anything, you're her teammate, not her adversary."

Emily stared at him, stunned and amazed. "Is that *really* how you see us?"

He nodded. "It is. So, what do you say, Miss Emily? You wanna see where this thing goes?"

Did she? Could she really trust her instincts after everything she'd been through in the last year? Could she really trust *him*?

"I…"

Dimitri bent and placed a tender kiss softly on her lips, and the touch of him soothed away all her uncertainty, like the tide washing clean the shore.

"…I really do," she said.

Epilogue

Six Months Later

DIMITRI LEANED IN the doorway and watched Emily finish teaching the beginners class to Lilly and some of her buddies from school.

Now that Ben was out on summer break, he had begun pitching in twice a week, too—and when class was done, he herded the little girls toward the door like a mallard with its ducklings. Being looked up to by so many of the smaller kids had done wonders for his self-confidence. He was like a different boy these days, and Dimitri knew the feeling.

Once all the parents had claimed their progeny, he and Emily and Lilly locked up for the night and began walking toward the car. As she usually did, Lilly asked Emily to join them for dinner—dangling a visit to the kitten Emily had gotten her for her birthday in the air like a real pro.

Dimitri was impressed by Lilly's flawless acting. Even though he'd drilled her for a week on what to say, her delivery was as normal and as natural as if she'd come up with it on the fly herself.

"You bet," Emily agreed readily. "That little furball is probably bigger already."

So far, so good. They all got in his car together and started driving toward home. They passed his and Lilly's old townhouse on the way, but no one even mentioned it—their new place had simply felt like home from the moment they'd moved in.

But then, Dimitri's carefully choreographed plan for the evening began unravelling. Lilly started begging Emily to stay over for another sleepover, and that *wasn't* one of her lines. If his kid gave too much away too soon, Emily was going to suspect something was up. Dimitri really, really wanted her to be surprised, though.

He launched into a completely fictional account of the kitten's antics from the night before. His daughter was successfully distracted, and he managed to get them home without Emily guessing a thing. Once they stepped into the family room, however, there'd be no hiding the surprise any longer.

Emily spotted the huge arrangement of flowers and balloons right away. She'd have had to be comatose not to.

"These are beautiful! What are they for?"

Dimitri shot Lilly a look—that was their cue. They both hopped into position, and when Emily turned back around, Dimitri was on one knee with Lilly beside him. True, his daughter was also trying to catch the kitten, who kept darting back and forth under their legs, but she was *mostly* ready.

Emily's face went slack with shock. They had her, all right.

"Guys? What are you doing?" She grabbed vaguely for the chairback next to her and hung on for dear life.

"Emily, we have a big *por-por-sal* for you," Lilly intoned solemnly. She grabbed for the cat's tail again, but thankfully missed.

"What?" Emily's knees buckled slightly, and Dimitri figured he'd better get on with it before she passed out on them.

He asked, "Maybe instead of a sleepover, you'd like to stay. Permanently."

"Will you marry me?" Lilly inquired quickly, in her high, sweet voice.

He smiled down at his kid, even though she'd upstaged him and stolen his line. To Emily, he repeated, "Will you marry *us*?"

"Are you serious?" she squeaked. She blinked furiously, but it didn't do much to stem the tears welling up in her aquamarine eyes.

"It's okay," Lilly chirped, unconcerned. "Mommy said she'll be your guardian angel, so you'll always know what to do."

"Oh my God," Emily murmured to herself. "She did?"

Dimitri had stopped being surprised when Lilly made comments like that. Either Anna had truly decided to take a firm position on this union from beyond the grave, or Lilly had developed the quirk as a way to cope with her evolving family life. Either way, it was all good—as long as they got to keep Emily.

Dimitri got to his feet and went to her, folding Emily's diminutive frame into his arms. She collapsed bonelessly against him, while Lilly anchored her around the thighs.

"Please?" he whispered against her hair.

"Are we sure about this?" Emily wondered, her words muffled in his t-shirt.

"Yes, Emily," Lilly piped up, "We are."

As peanut galleries went, Dimitri hoped his daughter was getting high marks for cuteness. Especially when she pried Emily's hand from his waist and handed it up to him.

He nodded at her and pulled the ring from his pocket. He jumped the gun a bit and slipped it onto Emily's finger, then had to swallow hard at the way her hand trembled in his.

Emily stroked his daughter's head, and gasped when she looked at her ring finger, now sporting a sparkling rock it had taken Dimitri exactly three-point-five seconds to pick out. It was *that* perfect for her.

"I love you guys," she said, voice wavering.

"She said yes!" Lilly cried, letting go to cavort around the room, and startling the kitten into a mad, sliding dash across the hardwood floor.

"Not quite," Dimitri chuckled, gazing down at the woman he loved.

Emily frowned. "Yes, I did," she argued.

"Well…" Dimitri hedged.

"Say it, say it, say it," chanted the little imp he'd somehow sired.

"Yes!" Emily laughed. "Of course, yes. How could I possibly refuse you two nuts? You'd never let me hear the end of it."

"That's true," he agreed. "But only because we want you and need you so much."

Emily just sighed and kissed him.

It wasn't the world's most romantic proposal, Dimitri supposed, but that hardly mattered. Against all odds, he'd managed to find happiness again—to find love, again—and that was more than good enough for him.

Forever Starts Now

A Lost & Found Short Story

Kristen Casey

Chapter One

Mina

"THIS WAS A horrible mistake," Mina said, looking around.

They'd made it from the Eastern Shore to the airport in Baltimore with no trouble, and the flight itself had been three hours of clear skies and zero turbulence. Now that she and Mack were making their way through the Wilmington baggage claim terminal, though, she couldn't shake her feeling of dread.

"Mina don't say that. Come on. It'll be fun," Mack argued. He knocked her shoulder with his, and Mina had to sidestep quickly to avoid tripping over someone's baby stroller.

"But what if no one remembers me?" she asked. "What if they're all still mad at me for not keeping in touch?"

"You're whining," Mack pointed out calmly. He examined the overhead signs, found the carousel that was supposed to spit out their luggage, and dragged her by the hand over to it.

"I *know*," Mina moaned. "But I don't think I've ever been so nervous to see people in my life."

"I get it. But that's not a good reason to miss your little sister's baby shower."

"Says you," she grumbled.

"Right. Says me. And...also that man." Mack pointed at a guy near the doors, holding a handmade sign that read "MINA" in big bold letters.

"That's Jake," she confirmed. Her sister's husband was taller, tanner, and way more handsome than Mina remembered. All that O'Connell loving had apparently done wonders for him since the last time they'd met.

Mack lifted their bags from the conveyor belt and turned to stroll toward his future brother-in-law. With a grin and a wave, Jake came forward to meet them halfway.

"Hey man," Mack said, bumping fists with him. "Thanks for picking us up."

"No problem," Jake shrugged. "How was the flight?"

"Smooth sailing," her fiancé drawled.

Mina rolled her eyes—cue the bromance. "Jake, meet Mack. Mack, this is Molly's baby daddy, Jake."

Jake hooked his thumbs in his pockets and smirked, looking mighty proud of himself for that particular feat.

"Congratulations," Mack said.

"Thanks. We're really excited."

Mack added, "What's a dude gotta do to get in that fix, anyway? I've been…"

"Where *is* Molly, anyway?" Mina wondered loudly.

Jake laughed. "She had to hit the head, for about the hundredth time since we got here." He indicated the ladies room nearby, then jammed his hands deep in his pockets while they watched the line of women streaming in and out.

"Jake, why'd they have to go and invite Elaine to this thing?" Mina complained. "Was that really necessary?"

"Oh, *right*," he snorted. "Like anyone was going to tell your mom she couldn't come."

Mina scowled, knowing the truth of that comment. "I suppose," she admitted grudgingly. "It's still going to be weird, though. I mean—Mom in the same room as Dad's new wife? That's bonkers."

"Yep. You're probably right," he agreed.

Mack elbowed her and murmured slyly, "It's like your family specialty!"

At last, Molly came rushing out, flushed and sweating and wiping her hands on her shorts. Mina gaped at her.

"Oh, my Lord," she muttered. Her sister's belly had doubled in size—at minimum—since the last time she'd seen her. Molly's ankles and feet looked quite a bit thicker than usual in her sandals, and she waddled a bit when she walked.

Her hair was still a thick and shining mass of glorious mahogany waves, though, and her brilliant smile was a mile wide.

"Meeny!" she sang, before barreling into her.

"Oof," Mina said, planting her feet so she wouldn't be bowled over. "Good grief. You're bigger than a barn, all of a sudden."

"Thank you for pointing that out. I missed you too," Molly snarled.

"All right," Jake interjected, quickly slinging an arm around his wife. "I figure we've got about twenty minutes to get you home before you're gonna have to pee again. Let's get these fine people in the car."

The couple led the way outside, passing through the sliding doors into a bank of humidity and cigarette smoke that hit Mina in the face like a brick wall. Her sister coughed and rapidly tucked her face into the collar of her frilly maternity shirt, but the damage was apparently already done.

They were only on the road long enough for Jake to pull away from the airport before things went south. Under her breath, Mina asked Mack once more if the baby shower games she'd pulled off the internet were going to be too dumb, and then her sister was hunched over and retching into a grocery bag between her knees.

Thankfully, Jake had warned Mina about this possibility. With a worried look at Mack, she leaned forward and waved around the air sickness bags she'd copped from the plane.

"You haven't quite gotten the hang of that southern hospitality thing, yet. Have you, Molls?" she murmured, patting her sister's back.

Molly yanked the little white paper bags from her hand and threatened, "Oh, just you wait. Your time will come."

Mina leaned back and smiled at Mack. "Sounds delightful," she said.

"Can't wait!" he beamed back, squeezing her thigh.

Jake turned the A/C up to full-blast, then shifted all the vents he could reach toward his wife. He turned the radio up, too—presumably so the country music would mask the sound of Molly's barfing.

"This is going to be great," Jake said, begging them with his eyes in the rearview mirror. "Isn't it, guys? Just as soon as we can get this girl home again, everything…is going to be…*great.*" He smoothed Molly's hair gently off her cheek and patted her shoulder.

Mina wasn't sure if he really meant what he said, or if his bold words were intended as an optimistic prayer of some sort. She simply grabbed Mack's hand and hung on—and tried not to take her sister's upset stomach as an omen of things to come.

Once they arrived at Jake and Molly's house, her sister immediately disappeared into her bedroom. Jake showed them around, then installed them in an airy guest room upstairs before disappearing himself.

Mina and Mack had barely begun unpacking when they heard the doorbell ring downstairs.

Mack said, "Uh-oh. I think that's my cue, kiddo."

"What are you talking about?" she asked, confused.

"I think Jake went to get your mom from her hotel. That's probably them now. He and I figured we'd go out for some burgers while you all catch up."

"Wait—what? When did you plan that?" Mina tried not to panic, but she'd thought she'd have at least a *little* more time before she had to socialize with Elaine.

"We arranged it on the phone," Mack told her, grabbing his wallet off the bureau. "You gonna be okay on your own?"

"No! I can't believe you're abandoning me!"

Mack just grinned at her, totally unmoved. "Trust me, it's for the best. You have fun, and I'll see you later."

"How much later?" Mina demanded.

"*Later*," he reiterated. Then, the betrayer dropped a casual kiss on her cheek and strolled out.

Mina stared at his retreating back in utter disbelief. When "later" finally rolled around, she was going to kill him—and it looked like she'd have plenty of time to plan how she was going to do it.

Morgan

SHE AND OWEN had barely landed in Boston with the kids, jet-lagged and exhausted after the long trip from New Zealand, before her sister Meg had muscled Morgan back onto a plane for the short flight down to North Carolina. On the one hand, she missed Owen, Ollie, and Katie with a gnawing ache behind her breastbone that she couldn't seem to get rid of. But on the other, it was great to be divested of all their stuff and sticky hands and constant needs—to remember what she'd been like before she became a mom.

Morgan thought she might be slightly delirious from the freedom. She couldn't wait to see the O'Connell sisters and all their friends and family, despite the very real possibility that Mina and Molly might not even remember her. Frankly, it had been so long since she'd had a legitimate girls' night out, that Morgan would probably have happily tagged along to *any* random woman's bachelorette party. The fact that it was a surprise for Mina O'Connell—a woman she'd met exactly one time but had always felt a real affinity for—simply made this getaway better.

As for the baby shower tomorrow morning, well…sometimes sisters had to do things for their sisters. Meg wouldn't have missed Molly's shower for the world, so here they were.

After Jake and Molly had dropped them off hours earlier, she and Meg had checked into Mrs. Denson's adorable little B&B. They'd had plenty of time to settle in, but her little sister was still flustered and spazzing out, trying to get herself ready for Mina's hen party that evening.

Morgan didn't think she'd been *quite* that out of it when her kids were babies, but maybe the twin thing was to blame. Meg was a hot mess.

Somewhere in their room, a text dinged on her sister's phone. Meg dove for her bed and dug through the discarded outfits covering it, before declaring, "She's there! We gotta go!"

"Great," Morgan smiled. "Let's hit it." She was so ready to get her wine on, it wasn't even funny.

"But I'm not ready," Meg cried. "My hair is still wet, and I can't find any lipstick. I think I forgot it."

"You look fine," she assured her. "Just put your hair up. We're only going to be sitting around Molly's living room—it's not like you're meeting the queen or anything."

"I know. But I haven't met some of the other ladies coming. I want to make a good impression."

"Okay, first, you've probably never made a bad impression in your life. And second, if these women are friends of Molly's, my guess is they are all going to be nice people. They won't care what you look like."

Meg stood there blinking at her, like she was having troubling processing that simple information.

"Come on," Morgan urged her. "We'll tell them you have 'twin syndrome,' get a glass of wine in you, and you'll feel much better."

Meg's brow furrowed. "Do you think I should be drinking booze? If I didn't leave enough breast milk for Edward, they might run out."

"If they run out, then the girls will have to drink formula for a little while. They'll live, I promise. Besides, it's done now—nothing you can do from down here, except to make sure you have a good time."

Her sister took a deep breath. "Okay. Here goes nothing—I hope Mina likes surprises."

MEG DROVE THEM the short distance to Molly's house in their rented coupe and parked on the tree-lined street out front. In the driveway, Jake was helping an older woman out of the passenger seat of his shiny black car.

"Front door's open," he called. "Head on in, and we'll see you gals later, okay?"

Before they could move, though, the front door swung wide, and a tall, good-looking man with dark hair and broad shoulders came trotting down the porch steps. He greeted the woman in the driveway with a hug, then stood and waited for Morgan and Meg to approach.

Jake said, "Mack, this is Molly's friend Meg, and her sister Morgan. They just got in this morning."

"Hey, thanks for coming, you guys," the man said. "I know Mina will appreciate it."

"And this is Molly and Mina's mom, Elaine," Jake told them.

The woman was wearing a metallic gray dress last seen in the Eighties, and enough lipstick to choke a horse. She extended her manicured hand with a regal, "Nice to meet you."

Meg was digging around in her handbag, so Morgan stepped forward to do the honors.

Behind them, her sister finally extracted the tube of lip gloss she'd been hunting for. "Yes!" she cried triumphantly, then sheepishly moved in to shake hands as well.

Morgan rolled her eyes. "Will you stop? You look fine!"

"But *look* at her," Meg muttered under her breath. "I'm totally underdressed."

"Okay, we're out," Jake told them, laughing. "Have fun, ladies!"

Mack gave them an amused wave, too, then the men ducked into Jake's car and backed rapidly down the driveway. They pulled away a bit quicker than was probably necessary under the circumstances, but who knew what had been going on inside that house all day.

The front door flew open once more, to reveal Molly—in all her flushed, hugely pregnant glory.

"Thank God you're here," she told them, waving her hands. "Hurry up and get inside. Mina's still in her room, so we might have a few minutes to set up before she comes down."

They hadn't even reached the porch before a woman—who could only be the guest of honor—appeared behind Molly in the foyer.

"Molly?" she asked, after looking around at the assembled faces warily. "What's going on?"

Two more cars rolled up slowly, parked one after another in the driveway, then ejected three more stylish women in various types of sundresses and dressy sandals. Meg blinked, took down her hair, fluffed it around, then re-wound it into another, identical knot on the back of her head.

Molly scanned the crowd and sighed, "Okay, I think that's everyone. Looks like we'll be setting things up together."

Seven women turned as one to smile widely at Mina. It was apparent that she was…a bit concerned about what might be occurring.

"Welcome to your bachelorette party!" Molly laughed, throwing her arms around her sister.

Their mom bustled up to them, pulling sparkling things from a plastic shopping bag dangling from her arm.

"Surprise!" she sang, then wedged herself between her daughters to drape a satin "Bride" sash across Mina. Elaine jammed a plastic tiara on Mina's head, arranged her daughter's hair around it, then stepped back.

"*Now*, we're ready," she claimed.

Molly spirited her befuddled sister back into the depths of the house with a flurry of whispered reassurances. Elaine stationed herself in the front hall, to drape glittering feather boas on each of the women as they passed. In short order, the bevy of guests had commandeered Molly's kitchen and family room—some laying out platters of finger foods, some hanging decorations, some bickering over the musical selections.

Morgan busied herself with setting out the wineglasses and punch cups where Molly directed her, then watched from the sidelines as each of the women made their way over to the bride-to-be, introducing themselves and offering happy congratulations. Mina looked staggered and overwhelmed but accepted the attention with reasonable good grace, all things considered.

She kept trying to help, though—and finally Molly was forced to park her sister on the sofa and demand that she stay put. Someone passed Mina a plate of snacks, and another handed her wine, but neither seemed to be doing the trick.

As expected, Morgan's own sister had loosened up quite nicely once she'd downed a few gulps of Merlot. Meg then attempted to convince Molly that a sip or two of wine wouldn't hurt her or the baby, without much success. She paused in her campaign only to ask Morgan to sit with the disgruntled honoree, to keep Mina company while everyone else finished getting ready for the party.

Morgan sidled around two women concocting something very pink and fruity-smelling in a huge crystal punch bowl, then joined Mina on the couch.

"Hey, remember me?" she smiled, trying to tamp down her sudden nerves.

Mina's grin was incandescent, though a tad watery. "Of course, I do. God, Morgan, you look exactly the same. Don't you age?"

"Uh, yeah, and you're just being sweet. But love *definitely* agrees with you. How are you holding up?"

"Okay. I guess."

"Despite being put in a time out?" Morgan laughed.

Mina snorted. "I was, wasn't I? I feel so useless right now. Why can't I help?"

"House rules. Besides, you'll get your chance tomorrow," Morgan said. "Do you think Molly knows she's getting her own party, too?"

"Doubtful," the other woman shrugged. "If I know my sister, she's been too busy barfing and trying to keep this secret from *me*, to even consider the fact that it's also the perfect time for us to throw her a baby shower."

Morgan eyed Molly across the room and could easily believe it. "Has she been very sick?"

"I get the impression that 'morning sickness' is a bit of a misnomer in her case."

"Ugh," Morgan shuddered. "I was like that with my second one. Went away by month five or so, though."

"I feel like I keep hearing stuff like that. Mack and I were going to start trying as soon as we got married, but now I'm starting to wonder if it's a good thing that the wedding's taking so long to plan." As if she'd suddenly remembered the wineglass balanced on her knee, Mina lifted it to her lips and drained half of it in one long swallow.

She continued, "Mack's getting antsy, though. And now that we're here and he's seeing all the baby craziness first hand, it's only going to get worse."

"That's kind of sweet," Morgan told her.

"Yeah. I know," Mina admitted, with a crooked little smile.

Morgan elbowed her, wanting to nudge the bride out of her funk. "You seem to be over-achieving by marrying a guy with an 'M' name, wouldn't you agree? Wasn't it enough to have just us girls be in the club?"

"He ate some of the candies you sent," Mina laughed. "I kind of had to."

Morgan thought about the dark and sexy man she'd met in the driveway earlier, and said, "Even if he hadn't, I think you probably still had to. Mack's pretty adorable."

"Oh, did you meet him?"

Mina seemed delighted when Morgan nodded.

"He just keeps getting cuter, too," she mused. "Even if he's about ready to frog-march me to the altar by now. I promised Mack we could throw something together in a few months, and it's taken twice that long." Mina asked her, "Did you have anything like that happen when you were getting married?"

Morgan had assumed Mina had heard the whole story by now, but apparently not. "Welllll…Owen and I sort of jumped the gun," she hedged. "We had a pretty quick shotgun deal, if you catch my drift."

When Mina's eyes bugged out a bit, she figured—in for a penny, in for a pound. "I have to say, it was not exactly the way I thought I'd meet my future in-laws." Morgan grinned. She missed them all so much already. Now that she had a home—a real one—it was hard to believe how much she hated to leave it.

"Oops," Mina giggled, leaning toward her conspiratorially.

Morgan was satisfied, though. Her awkward admission had definitely relaxed the other woman, who no longer seemed as nervous as she had before.

Looking around, it was clear that everyone had completed whatever tasks they'd been assigned, and the party was ready to begin in earnest. She put her arm around Mina and squeezed.

"You ready for this?" she asked.

Mina blew out a breath. "Nope. Not even a little bit," she confessed. "But that's never been a factor before."

Morgan chuckled. "Why start now?"

Chapter Two

Meg

IF EDWARD DIDN'T stop texting her about the twins' antics, Meg was going to lose her mind. She supposed her husband was doing it because he knew how uncomfortable she'd been about leaving them, even if it was just for the weekend. But she was already flustered trying to help Molly throw the no-longer-a-surprise party, and the regular chiming of her cell phone was only adding to her discombobulation. Besides, hearing all about how much fun the girls were having with their cousins only made her wish she was there to see it.

As if she knew exactly what was going through Meg's mind, her sister Morgan sidled up beside her, nipped the phone from her fingers, and dropped it behind them on the counter.

"No more of that," Morgan murmured. "We have a bachelorette to honor."

All around them, Molly's friends and family were piling food onto plates, passing around glasses of wine and punch, and parking themselves on chairs and ottomans around the room. Meg frowned over her sister's shoulder, watching as the bride's mother produced a large bottle of rum from somewhere and began pouring it into the punch.

"Tell Molly the punch is now off-limits," she said.

Morgan huffed, "Not a problem. I'm pretty sure she'd be mainlining ginger ale right now, if she could figure out how to do it politely."

Molly's sister-in-law joined them in the kitchen, and the petite brunette's eyes were glowing with excitement.

"Thanks for letting Shannon and me come!" she enthused. "This is way better than going out to some club and having weird guys skeeving on us all night!"

"Yeah, well, apparently we still have to worry about people slipping things into our drinks," Meg grumbled.

At Healey's startled expression, Morgan hastened to clarify, "Molly's mom just doctored your punch."

"Ah," the younger woman said. "It was bound to happen. Anyway, just wanted to let you know I stuck the rest of the baby shower decorations out in the garage. Jake showed me where everything else was."

Meg patted her on the back. "Thanks for that. The less we had to cart down on the plane, the better."

"No worries," Healey shrugged. "Come sit down. I think everyone has what they need for now. You two should take a load off."

Meg's sister tugged her toward the last two unoccupied chairs, handed her a fresh glass of wine, and turned to smile at the circle of happy faces.

From the seat of honor, Mina cleared her throat, obviously feeling obligated to say something. "Wow, you guys. This was really nice of you. I…can't quite believe we're actually doing this."

Molly cut in, "Oh, we're doing it. Mom, can you please turn the music down a bit?"

Elaine was perched on a barstool at the island separating the family room from the kitchen. She pouted but complied without comment.

Once she didn't have to talk so loudly, Molly continued, "I can't believe it's been so many years since we all went out in Boston that time. And not for nothing, but you girls—" She pointed her finger at Meg and Morgan, "—have been busy little bees since then."

"Really?" Mina looked around. "What happened?"

There was some general shifting around while people wise-cracked with their neighbors, but finally Morgan leaned forward to start explaining.

"Well, I got divorced," she said. Meg was relieved when her sister skipped over the miscarriage part, with only a quick glance at Molly's belly. Then Morgan continued, "Went on a trip, *stayed* there, and then fell for my boss. Who I was living with at the time."

Meg snorted at the hilariously truncated version of her sister's life. "Oh, is that all? You, like, got mixed up in some crazy international diamond-smuggling ring! There was murder and mayhem!"

"That was completely beside the point," Morgan stated primly.

"Was it?" Meg balked.

Mina looked a little shell-shocked, but she interjected, "What about you, Meg?"

Her sister was all over that, of course. "Ha," Morgan laughed. "Nothing major for her. She just married an earl-in-training, that's all."

"Edward's not like that," Meg protested.

Molly was supposed to be her best friend, but apparently felt the need to correct the record—like the good attorney she was.

"Pshh," she mocked, "Was that before or after the amnesia?"

Meg narrowed her eyes at her—Molly had just lost her new-mommy pass. "At least he never forgot to mention an inconvenient *fiancée*!"

"Low blow," Healey murmured.

Mina sat back and looked around. "Except for that last part, I have no idea what's going on right now," she said.

"In Jake's defense," Molly pointed out, "I never really gave him a chance to tell me about her."

Mina cocked her head, frowned comically, and told the other guests, "Okay, she's kind of rewriting history there."

Molly wasn't taking that jab laying down, though—she squawked, "Oh, you're one to talk!"

Morgan turned to Meg and muttered, "This oughta be good."

"It is," Meg replied. "Years ago, Mina's first husband apparently stole her from her current fiancé, but now that the jerk is dead, she and Mack can finally be together."

Molly's coworker Shannon, a lovely and elegant African-American woman, sat back in her armchair with wide eyes. "Whoa," she breathed, clearly impressed.

Morgan asked, "Are we allowed to talk about dead people like that?"

In unison, Meg and Molly belted out, "*Yes.*" And then she and her friend just sat there grinning at each other across the room like a couple of goofballs. Maybe Morgan was right, and the wine *had* been a good idea. Meg could already feel the tension in her shoulders seeping away.

Over on the sofa, the guest of honor squawked at her sister, "You *told* them that?"

"Of course," Molly shrugged. "Why wouldn't I?"

Meg's own sister tried to smooth things over, like she always did. Morgan smiled at Mina, "Have you not been paying attention for the last half hour? Between us, we have enough material for, like, a full week's worth of television talk shows here."

Not to be outdone, Mina and Molly's mother piped boozily up from her stool. "Hah! If you thought that was bad, wait till I tell you the rest—we found out later Grey was part of an international drug ring!"

Mina dropped her head into her hands and groaned loudly.

Meg turned to her sister. "Too bad he's dead," she told Morgan, "We could've fixed him up with your diamond felons."

Morgan snorted in amusement. "Right?" she chuckled.

Jake's sister Healey gazed at the gathering with an amazed expression. "I…I think I need to get out more," she mused.

Shannon shook her head and crossed her arms across her chest. "I've been telling you."

Molly watched the exchange between her coworker and her sister-in-law, then announced to the group, "And all this time, they thought *they* were living on the edge."

Meg was ready to have the focus on someone else for a while, so she asked her, "What did they do?"

Molly didn't have a chance to answer, though. Healey was more than happy to get out in front of her story. She raised her hand quickly and announced, "Snuck around behind my brother's back with his best friend."

"Yeah, Tim's *my* brother," Shannon explained. Then, when everyone continued to stare at her, she added, "Oh, I only had an extremely ordinary office affair."

Elaine was pouting again. "*Aw*," she whined.

"No, I'm good, actually," Shannon told her. "Completely cool with it."

Out of nowhere, an older woman Meg hadn't met bustled out of the kitchen, hoisted the punch bowl, and inquired, "More punch anyone?"

Meg squinted at her sister, wracking her brain to remember who this woman was. She must have been listening in from the kitchen the whole time.

Elaine snipped, "You aren't at work. Stop trying to serve everyone and sit down, will you?"

After Morgan shrugged, Meg turned to Molly, who was massaging her forehead with a pained expression. "I think everyone's had plenty. Thanks, Felice."

"Oh," Morgan whispered to her, eyes lighting up. "That's Molly and Mina's new stepmother!"

Right. Which explained why the girls' mother was acting testy with her. Molly's sister-in-law Healey rose and took the punch bowl from the woman with a nod. And together, they began walking the punch bowl around, so the ladies could refill their glasses.

"Can you ever really have too much punch?" Healey asked them.

Meg was beginning to wonder that very thing. She'd watched Elaine pour an entire bottle of rum into the concoction, and the truth was—the ladies *were* getting a bit giggly. Tipsy at a bachelorette party—who would've guessed?

SOMETIME LATER, MEG awoke to Morgan smoothing the hair gently back from her face.

"Meg's out. Apparently, you *can* have too much punch," her sister proclaimed.

"I'm awake," Meg protested groggily. "I'm fine." Had she actually fallen asleep in the middle of a bachelorette party? She'd better pray her husband's brothers didn't get wind of that—they'd never let her hear the end of it.

The doorbell rang, and Elaine shot off her seat. "Oh, good! He's finally here!" she squealed, clapping her hands and heading toward the door.

Everyone looked around, asking their companions, "*Who's* here?"

Molly and Mina's mother stalked grouchily back into the room, though, trailed by three impeccably dressed women that she obviously hadn't expected.

Molly bolted to her feet far more quickly than Meg would've thought her capable. "Mom?" she squeaked. "And Grandma Faye. And Aunt *Ceecee!*"

Morgan leaned in and muttered in her ear, "Now, who are they?"

"I think that's Jake's mom, Stella, and his grandma and great-aunt. Remember? Molly said this used to be Ceecee's house."

Meg watched Healey high-tail it across the room, too, where she began helping the two elderly women into a pair of recently-vacated chairs. She propped their canes in the corner next to them and fetched half-filled glasses of punch.

The ladies merrily clinked their cups, took hearty sips, then nodded in approval to each other. Healey settled her mother on one of the bar stools, poured her a glass of white wine, and hurried away.

Molly was waiting for her. Standing at Meg's elbow, she grabbed for the young woman's arm and hissed, "*Why* are they all here right now?"

Healey flushed guiltily. "I am so sorry," she whispered. "My mama overheard me talking about the party. I had to pretend like her invitation got lost, and I'll tell you what—I don't think wild dogs could've kept my grandma and Ceecee away."

Molly harrumphed, shot a wary glance at the new arrivals, and began rubbing her belly like she was making a wish.

Something peculiar had just occurred to Meg, though. "Wait," she said, pointing to Elaine. "You said before that *he* was finally here. Who, exactly, were you expecting?"

Molly

SHE MIGHT BE big and pregnant and hungry every moment she wasn't puking her guts out—but Molly was determined to fete her big sister Mina. The woman had been through way too much in her life to not have this one little rite of passage go her way.

But Molly had to question why on earth she'd thought inviting their mother Elaine was a good idea. From the moment the woman had landed in North Carolina, she'd been *way* too into it—but only in her typically self-absorbed way.

She'd spent the evening swanning around the room, dressed in a shiny wrap dress straight from the set of a nighttime soap opera, and jockeying for position with Felice, her ex-husband's new flame. Mina had been sniping at her, accusing her of acting weird. Naturally, their mom had gotten defensive, claiming she hadn't ever gotten to do any of the normal wedding things herself. If this was going to be her only shot, she was determined to go out with a bang.

All that was par for the course.

What worried Molly more was her mother's smug expression, and the jittery way she kept checking her hair and her lipstick and her watch. Molly hadn't even noticed Elaine's strange slip of the tongue before Meg pointed it out, but she had only moments to contemplate it before her doorbell was ringing once more.

Her mother skittered off, only to return leading an oddly tan and good-looking guy—wearing a hardhat, reflective vest, and baggy canvas pants—by the hand. She deposited him in the center of the family room carpet, and the room full of women fell silent.

"Hello, ladies," he announced. "I'm Jason, with the city of Wilmington. I heard you had a problem that needed fixing."

Across the room, Morgan giggled and started elbowing her sister to wake her up again. Molly edged into the room two steps, but no farther. She had a bad feeling about where this was going.

"Maybe something to do with your missing shirt?" Healey snickered, then balked when Shannon whacked her on the arm.

"Nooooo," the guy drawled, flexing and preening. "I heard there was a lady in this house about to get hitched." He nodded at Elaine, who pressed a button on a small set of speakers with an outsized flourish.

Grandma Faye was cackling like that revelation was the greatest joke in history. She poked at her sister Ceecee, who in turn raised a slightly-shaking finger to point out Mina.

"That's her!" she crowed over the thumping bass. Mina shrank into the loveseat and turned an alarming shade of crimson.

Elaine sashayed over to Molly with a grin, while the pseudo-laborer rolled his hips and began gyrating inches from Mina's lap.

"Mother, what on earth have you done?" Molly hissed at her.

"Isn't he terrific?" Elaine laughed giddily, "Look at him go!"

The man peeled off his neon vest and tossed it in Meg's direction, then set his hardhat on Mina's head before descending into a series of rolling thrusts that took him nearly to the floor at her feet. It didn't seem humanly possible to move that way—but perhaps he'd been born with some extra muscles or fewer bones than most men.

His theme music pulsated through the room, turning her brain to sludge. It took far too long for Molly's thoughts to churn out the critical information: Her mother had hired a male stripper for her own daughter's bachelorette party. She'd even managed to discover one who dressed as a construction worker, no doubt thinking Mina would enjoy that since Mack often wore a hardhat to work as a coastal engineer.

Dear Lord. Her sister looked like she wanted to disappear, or at minimum, crawl under the floorboards. Morgan and Meg were cracking up, shimmying comically in their seats in a younger echo of Faye and Ceecee's antics. Jake's mom stood stiffly near the kitchen, pretending not to sneak peeks at the dancer's admittedly impressive back.

When "Jason" straightened up—only to rip his canvas pants from his legs and swirl them in a circle around his head—Molly thought her sister-in-law was going to choke on her own tongue. Healey goggled at Jason's metallic g-string—striped orange and white like a traffic cone—then did a spit-take worthy of any television comedy routine. Molly didn't think she'd ever *seen* her coworker Shannon laugh so hard. She was beginning to fear for the woman's well-being.

"Whoa, whoa, whoa," Molly bellowed, trying to march into the room to stop the guy. Her mother yanked her back.

"Oh no you don't," Elaine scolded. "No need to worry. It's not like he's going to take it *all* off."

Molly struggled to understand how this could have happened. Having the party here at the house—instead of out at some rowdy club—was supposed to *prevent* something like this. She should have known their mom would find some way to run the whole operation off the rails. Mina was never going to forgive her.

Across the room, Healey had moved to perch on the arm of Ceecee's chair and was snickering so hard she was crying. The dancer continued on with his routine, hamming it up and seemingly oblivious to the reactions of the women he was entertaining.

Out of nowhere, Morgan's voice rose above the din. "What the heck are you doing?" she cried. "*Recording* this?"

Meg was offended. "No!" she screeched back. "I'm conferencing Poppy." She beamed goofily at her phone screen and belted out, "Poppy, I can't believe you're missing this! You would *love* it!" And then, after a brief pause, she added, "Oh! Hi, George! Look—this guy dresses just like you!"

Morgan slapped a hand over the cell phone screen. "Put that away right now," she scolded her sister. "Honestly."

"Party pooper," Meg grouched, before signing off with a forlorn, "Sorry guys, gotta go. The sheriff is cracking down."

Molly felt a horrified chuckle slip out at that exchange—but immediately bit down on her lip to stifle it, lest her mother think she was on board with this insane idea. Over on the rug, Jason tried mightily to get a couple of the younger women out of their seats to gyrate with him but kept getting waved off.

He gave Molly a bit of a scare when he marched in her direction, but she should have known he wouldn't want any part of a mother-to-be the size of a whale. He merely winked at her, grabbed Elaine, and hauled her to the center of the room. Not to be outdone in the spectacle department, her mom somehow managed to collar Felice, too—creating the world's most awkward mother/stripper sandwich.

More than one attendee flinched, but quick-thinking Mina took the opportunity to leap from her seat and bolt across the room toward Molly. Her sister clutched her arm like a panicked animal, watching the trio whoop and writhe mere feet away.

Molly mused, "What do you suppose Dad would say about—"

"Uh-uh. Nope. Do *not* finish that sentence," Mina warned.

It took an eternity, but at last Jason finished up, dipping first Elaine, then Felice toward the floor, and dropping what Molly assumed were meant to be seductive kisses on the hands of Faye and Ceecee. He snared Stella by the shoulders as he passed, landing a very enthusiastic kiss right on her unwilling mouth before he slipped out of sight and his music ended.

There was a smattering of applause, and not a few lewd jokes traded around. Her guests pushed to their feet and began straightening up in a disorganized and haphazard way. The fact that they all seemed to find everything hilarious made Molly wonder exactly how tipsy everyone had gotten. When she peeked at it, she found the punch bowl empty and swathed in Jason's road-crew vest. Oh. *That* tipsy.

Molly stepped into the kitchen to find a much different Jason, all business and waiting to get paid. Healey and Shannon were giggling and chatting him up—and trying to get his contact information for future bachelorette parties.

Molly shooed them off but didn't *quite* manage to get rid of the stripper before Jake and Mack came home. It figured.

Mina's fiancé was the first through the mudroom door, taking the measure of the stranger in one quick, all-encompassing glance. "Who the fu—" he began.

Jake pushed in beside him and held up a hand. "Do I know you?" he demanded.

Jason ducked his head, far less comfortable flaunting his pecs in front of his peers. "Naw, man," he mumbled shakily.

Molly grabbed blindly for the check her mother was trying to hand the guy and shoved it into Jason's fingers. "Okay, my mom paid you. You're good? We're all good?"

He examined the paper he held, but he was dubious. "Yeah, but she, like, wrote me a *check*. Is it gonna clear?"

Molly took him by his sweaty, strangely-slick bicep. Had he *oiled* himself? *Gross.*

"Yup!" she chirped, "Definitely gonna clear." Then she man-handled him out the front door before her husband could get ahold of him. "Okay, thank you. Goodbye!"

Jason ducked into a sad little hatchback parked at the curb, rusted and missing its hubcaps. With a loud backfire that would surely wake her neighbors, the stripper drove away.

Jake rested his chin on Molly's shoulder and wound his arms around her nonexistent waist.

"I think that dude might work with Tim," he commented.

Behind them, Felice approached and made a dismissive sound. "That may be true, but I *know* he works at my restaurant, and let me tell you what—I am *really* looking forward to my next shift."

Chapter Three

Morgan

MORGAN WAS YANKED from an odd and disturbing dream—involving an indecipherable plot to poison her, gyrating men, and the Queen of England—by the shrieking wail of the alarm. The clock was a clunky, retro plastic thing—and it was ludicrous that it had enough power to emit such a hideous noise.

Clearly, the alarm had been set by the prior guests, since neither she nor her sister had been in any shape to think of such a thing when Mack had dropped them off in the wee hours of the morning. They'd barely been capable of changing into their pajamas—and likely owed the B&B's proprietor an apology for all their giggling and stumbling around.

On the other bed, Meg had her pillow pressed tightly over her head, and might have been whimpering pathetically—it was hard to tell, over the squealing racket.

Morgan tried to figure out how to turn the darn thing off, but it was hard to ignore the screeching long enough to be able to think straight. After only a few tortured seconds, she resorted to yanking the cord from the wall.

Blissful silence blanketed their room, and Morgan heaved a sigh of relief. Now that she could hear her own thoughts, it became plain that her skull had been broken apart by a sledgehammer. If the wounded sounds coming from Meg were any indication, her sister felt the same.

On the nightstand, Morgan's phone began chirping with an incoming call. She glanced at the screen—*Owen*. Right on schedule, damn him. Why did her husband always have to be so punctual?

After some innocuous back-and-forth about the weather up in Boston, her husband declared, "Sweetheart, whatever you do in the next twenty-four hours, do *not* miss that flight back up here tomorrow."

"Why? Is everything okay?" Morgan tried to sit up, but the room spun crazily around her.

"Oh, it's fine. Ollie and Kate are having a ball. But I have learned something very important about myself in your absence."

She could tell by his tone that he was working up to a flirt. "Really," she said. "And what is that, pray tell?"

"It turns out that I *despise* sleeping by myself," he said, his voice filled with wonder.

"Oh, Owen. Me, too. It's awful, isn't it?"

"It is. Which is why you need to get back here soon," he said. "Please? I miss you."

Morgan promised him, "First thing tomorrow. I swear."

"I'll be here waiting, love. You can count on it."

Once they hung up, she knew she'd better pry herself out of bed and attempt to get cleaned up—she was liable to fall back asleep if she didn't. Meg had gone to sleep again, so Morgan crept into the bathroom as quietly as she could and took a long, hot shower. It helped a little with her headache, but not enough. She still felt sore and overheated as she zipped herself into the long maxi dress she'd brought for the occasion.

When she cracked the door to the bedroom, though, her own woes were forgotten. Meg had awoken after all, and was hunched over her mattress cursing and crying, trying to wrap Molly's baby shower gift.

Strewn across the bed were a number of new diapers and rolls of ribbon that Morgan assumed were the ill-fated remains of Meg's planned baby shower decoration—the ever-popular, three-layer diaper cake. Evidently, the actual assembly had proved far more difficult than the internet instructions had made it seem.

Or, maybe they were both so hungover that they might as well still be drunk—or dead. Come to think of it, dead might be the preferable option.

"Meggie, why don't you take a break and go grab a nice shower?" Morgan suggested. "You'll feel better, I promise."

Her sister slunk into the bathroom without a word of protest, so Morgan examined the various things on the bed while she towel-dried her hair. After a while, she sank to the mattress to try her hand at the diaper cake—despite her trembling fingers, aching head, and persistent nausea.

Seriously—it couldn't be natural for every blink of her eyes to thunder through her brain like a stampede of bison. How was aspirin supposed to tackle agony like that? How was she going to get through the morning's baby shower without everyone knowing she was a total mess?

Morgan found the wastebasket under the delicate antique writing desk. It was too pretty by half, especially considering the fact that if her little sister didn't exit the bathroom soon, Morgan was going to find herself face-first in its decoupaged depths. There'd be no explaining *that* to good Mrs. Denson.

Behind the bathroom door, she heard the sound of running water, but also the sound of some ghastly, sisterly retching. No relief from that quarter, then. Morgan curled onto her side, clutched the trashcan to her chest, and tried to take very, very shallow breaths.

She hoped like hell that her dress wouldn't wrinkle too badly. They were due at Molly's in less than an hour.

Within a few minutes, Morgan knew she'd have to concede defeat on every front. She sat up and swept the components of Meg's failed party "cake" into a shopping bag, in the hopes that one of the other women would be able to transform ordinary diapers into a Pinterest-worthy centerpiece.

Then, she stood and tried the door to the bathroom—locked. Scanning the room, Morgan spied the dry-cleaning bag she'd left draped across her suitcase earlier. She grabbed it, tied a knot in the top, and lined the wastebasket with it.

Resigned to the inevitable, she perched on the corner of the bed, spread her damp towel across her lap, and gripped the trash bin under her chin—and let nature take its painful course.

SOME TIME LATER, Morgan awoke to the feeling of someone gently rubbing circles on her back. It seemed too much to hope that it was Owen, given that her husband was supposed to be up in Boston with their children and Meg's family.

She cracked an eye and found her sister sitting beside her. Meg's hair and makeup were all done, though her sister *did* still look a bit green around the gills. Her face was a study in sympathy—Morgan must have fallen asleep after tossing her cookies.

"How are you feeling?" Meg inquired.

"I don't understand what's wrong with us," Morgan moaned. "I didn't think we drank that much last night."

"Combination of cheap rum and not enough dinner, I imagine," her sister replied sagely.

"You're probably right," Morgan agreed. "Unless—you don't think that dancer guy slipped us something, do you?"

Her baby sister didn't even dignify that with an answer. Instead, Meg asked, "Listen, do you think you can get up and blow dry your hair now? I'll be right back, I swear."

Morgan shoved upright, and the room stayed mostly stationary. "Where are you going?"

"I think Mrs. Denson probably has breakfast laid out by now. I'm going to go down and see if I can grab us some coffee and dry toast. Hopefully that will settle our stomachs enough to endure the car ride over to Molly's."

"Okay."

"I don't think there's any way I can stomach one of those scones Molly told us about," Meg said sadly. "Supposedly they're really good."

Morgan cringed at the thought. "Maybe she'll box a couple of them up for us."

Her sister snorted and eyeballed the erstwhile contents of Morgan's stomach, encased in plastic and set carefully on the tile threshold near the door, in case the bag leaked. The clear jerry-rigged sack revealed an unfortunate amount of detail.

"I'll ask Mrs. Denson for a trash bag, too," she said. "So we can dump *that* in the Dumpster out back when we leave. I'm sorry I hogged the bathroom before."

"S'okay," Morgan murmured dejectedly. It was gross. *She* was gross.

"Give me five minutes," Meg said, pushing to her feet. Despite her fancy clothes, she was moving like a little old lady.

"Megs?" she asked.

"Hmm?"

"Thank you. For everything."

"That's what sisters do," Meg said. "And I have a feeling that there's another pair of them across town who could use our help this morning."

Morgan had a sudden, concerning thought. "Speaking of which, how the heck are we supposed to get over there? Didn't Mack bring us home last night? I think we left our car at Molly's."

"Wait…" Meg's face scrunched up as she thought. "I vaguely remember something about Jake following us, so they could leave our car here with us. Do you remember which car we rode in?"

"Not a clue," Morgan admitted.

"I'll check the parking lot and see if it's there," Meg sighed heavily. "And I am never going to another party again."

"Except the one this morning," Morgan clarified.

"Yeah, well—at this rate that remains to be seen."

Molly

MOLLY SPENT FAR longer in bed that morning than she'd intended, but after the late night and all the residual party-planning stress, she'd slept even worse than usual. Her lower back was killing her, and she despised the way that made her shuffle around.

She'd managed to nibble on a few crackers without her morning sickness flaring up, though, so she supposed that was a minor victory. Even better was the sight of Mack and Jake in the kitchen, making pancakes and bacon, and joking around with each other like they'd been buddies for years. It boded well for future visits with her sister, and for many happy holidays spent together.

The food smelled delicious—for now. Too bad Molly was likely to upchuck it at any minute, given how unpredictable her stomach had been lately. She peeked over the island and found a veritable feast laid out on the counter. The guys had made way too much. Hopefully they planned on eating most of it, since Molly had serious doubts her sister would be able to help much either.

After about twenty minutes, Mina staggered into the room, clutching her skull like it might split apart. *Yup*…that was about what Molly had expected after the way the bachelorette party had ended. Molly dropped the box of painkillers she'd carried downstairs onto the counter and turned toward her sister.

"Why is the sun so freaking bright down here?" Mina whined. "It's like laser beams, trying to stab out my eyeballs."

Mack smirked. "Oooooh yeah," he drawled. "You should totally drink rum punch more often. You look fresh as a daisy right now."

"Shhhh," his future wife hissed. "We don't say the word *rum* today. Maybe ever again."

Molly rolled her eyes. "Aren't you being a little dramatic?"

"Says the woman whose mother poisoned the punch."

"She's your mother, too."

"Not anymore," her sister groaned.

Car doors slammed outside, and before Molly could move a muscle, Morgan and Meg let themselves in the front door. They, too, looked decidedly worse for wear.

"Hey ladies," Mack called. "Who's hungry? We have pancakes, bacon, coffee, orange juice…"

Morgan slapped a hand over her mouth and went pale.

Meg simply moaned, "No thank you," before scuttling over to Mina and slumping onto the couch next to her.

Jake snorted and shot a sly look at Mack. "Well, how about some scrambled eggs, then? Or I could make you a protein smoothie that my buddy Tim swears by. Raw eggs, kale, spinach, bananas…" he said.

Morgan emitted a faint gagging sound and turned even whiter. Over on the couch, Meg hid her face behind a throw pillow, but otherwise stayed silent. Mina gave her a forlorn sort of pat on the shoulder, then covered her eyes with her hand again.

Molly reached over the island and whacked her husband on the arm. "Stop it," she scolded. "Now you're just being cruel."

To the assorted women, she called, "Come in here, you guys. There's coffee and ibuprofen on the counter, if you want."

No one moved. Only a sudden barrage of loud rapping on the back door broke the deathly quiet—and then Healey spilled in, struggling with a teetering stack of fancy bakery boxes, as well as an unwieldy arrangement of pink and blue balloons.

"What the hell?" Molly wondered, examining the display.

Tim muscled in after his fiancée, bearing a steaming bag of fresh bagels, and his customary thousand-watt grin. "Baby girl has the hangover of the century," the hulking man announced. "Hey brother," he murmured to Jake, bumping fists.

Jake introduced Tim to Mack, and Molly watched as her sister's fiancé took in everything from Tim's crisp blue paramedic uniform to his enormous size. She was so used to her husband's best friend by now, that she hardly ever stopped to consider how other people saw him anymore. With that broad chest and those dark biceps straining his shirtsleeves, Molly could see where Tim might be…daunting. Neither Jake nor Mack were short guys, but Healey's man still towered over them by a few inches.

Mack seemed unperturbed, though, and Molly shouldn't have been surprised—so far, he'd handled everything about his and Mina's visit with the same easy-going aplomb. He was simply a joy to be around.

Tim looked over the assembled ladies with an amused expression wreathing his face.

"Uh, not for nothin'," he commented, "But the folks at the station would probably enjoy those bagels a heck of a lot more than the collection of walking wounded you all got up in here."

Healey smacked his hand away from the brown bag, though. "Tim, I *told* you to get two bags, but you didn't. Now, you'd better get out of here before you make yourself late for work."

He shook his head, bent to plant a loud, wet kiss on Healey's cheek, and ruffled her hair. "Be good, honey," Tim told her. "Or is it already too late for that?"

Healey scowled. "Have I ever told you how much I despise cheerful people in the morning?"

"Not in the last five minutes or so."

"Will you *leave* already?" she wailed.

"All right, I see how it is. Maybe you can call me later, once you've seen the error in your ways," he said.

"Maybe I will, and maybe I won't," Healey muttered sullenly.

With a good-natured laugh, Tim let himself out, while Molly marveled at what foul moods her friends were in. True, it had been a good long while since she'd suffered through a hangover, but seriously—this was ridiculous. *She* had an entirely new human being sitting on her bladder, but she still managed to crack a smile now and then.

Healey stared at her feet for a mere three seconds before fumbling for the back door. "Tim! Wait!"

He ducked his head back in, as if he'd been expecting exactly that request. They really were a perfect match, Molly mused.

"Forget anything?" he inquired.

"I love you," Healey said, kissing him gently on the cheek. "And I'm sorry."

"Love you, too, sweet girl. I'll catch you later, okay?"

Jake didn't bother tormenting his little sister with offers of eggs or weird shakes. He simply poured her a mug of black coffee and handed it over. Molly was getting ready to ask about the balloons again, when the doorbell chimed at the front door of the house. Geez Louise—it was like a tennis match that morning.

Molly hurried over and discovered Elaine and Felice loitering on her front porch. As soon as she opened the panels wide, the unlikely duo marched silently past, arms laden with chilled bottles of champagne and grapefruit juice. Molly opened her mouth to ask what in the world they were doing there—*together*—but was distracted by another car idling at the curb in front of her house.

A distinguished-looking gentleman in tortoiseshell glasses sat behind the wheel, and he looked awfully familiar. Sucking face with him, like the world might be ending later that day, was Shannon, her friend from the firm.

Molly blinked. That meant the driver was Molly's *other* coworker Vijay. Had Shannon actually ever made it home the night before, or had she simply sat out there making out with her boyfriend all night?

Molly didn't have much time to wonder, though, because Jake's mom pulled into her driveway with a worrying lurch of her brakes.

Stella rolled down her window to demand, "Molly, dear, send the boys out here if you will. Faye and Ceecee need some help getting up those stairs."

Molly spun around, confused, but Jake and Mack were already edging past her in the doorway and trotting down the porch steps. They extracted the two little old ladies from the back seat of Stella's car, and—after a flurry of polite apologies and lilac-scented kisses—they escorted them inside. An embarrassed and flustered Shannon brought up the rear, and then the entire horde of unscheduled, unexpected guests moved toward the back of the house.

Molly trailed after them and stood watching a slapdash production unfold that was eerily similar to the events of the night before. Only this time, she didn't seem to have a say in things—everyone was wandering around her like she wasn't even there.

When she couldn't take it a second longer, Molly screeched, "Will someone *please* explain what is going on right now? Why are you all back here again?"

Mina stopped in front of her, glowering and gesturing with a roll of masking tape in her hand. "This is what's called payback, little sister. Welcome to your baby shower."

Molly's mouth dropped open. Suddenly, it *was* looking a lot like a party. They couldn't be serious.

"Oh my God," she cried. "You've got to be kidding me. None of you are in any condition to throw a baby shower. Look at yourselves!"

Morgan swept past, holding a tiered tray of beautiful little cupcakes that Molly was reasonably sure no one would be able to stomach. "And yet, here we are," the woman grumbled, "Soldiering on."

The dogs scampered after her, bumping into each other and against Morgan's legs, causing the woman to stumble and curse under her breath.

Jake and Mack had arranged the elderly women on a pair of armchairs near the center of the room and were engaged in taking their coffee orders. Molly's mother-in-law supervised nearby, and naturally, Stella was exquisitely turned out in a pale blue linen suit and strappy stiletto-heeled sandals. She'd made a game effort to counteract how wan she was with a generous dose of blush and rosy lip gloss, but the result lacked its usual finesse. Molly winced. The last time Stella had looked that brittle had been the morning after Molly and Jake's wedding.

The Flynn sisters were beside her, deep in conference. Too loud, Morgan whispered, "How is that woman wearing heels? I'm pretty sure I could fall off a pair of flip-flops if I tried right now."

Meg shrugged. "I have no bloody idea. That's some pro-level adulting right there."

Morgan snorted in agreement. "And just think—*your* mother-in-law is a freaking countess. You'd think you'd be used to stuff like that by now."

"Nope," Meg said. "That is an act of valor even Violet might have trouble pulling off."

Molly shook her head in amazement. "This is completely crazy," she announced loudly to everyone, and no one.

Jake popped up beside her, with a restraining hand tucked into each dog's collar. Duke and Lolly panted happily up at her, pink icing streaking their jowls. Molly pulled out her phone and took a quick photo—they looked adorable, even if Healey was probably about to kill them for eating her cupcakes.

"Seems about right," Jake agreed cheerfully, then dragged the two mutts toward the mud room.

Over near the kitchen, her dad's wife was attempting to play some music—peppy reggae by the sound of it. Felice was roundly booed by the crabby women nearby, causing Elaine to step in and adjust the radio station to some more-soothing classical music.

Molly laughed. She'd never seen ten women less inclined to celebrate the birth of a baby before in her life.

She snagged a cold bottle of water from the arrangement that had sprouted up on her kitchen island, then strolled across the room, picking a seat halfway between the growing pile of prettily-wrapped presents and the downstairs bathroom. Healey plopped an errant tiara from the night before onto Molly's head, snapped a few pictures of her, and then whistled loudly through her teeth.

"All right, people—let's do this!" she bellowed.

It looked like another party—such as it was—was about to begin.

Chapter Four

Meg

S HE'D NEVER WITNESSED anything quite like the roomful of women crowding her best friend's family room, all hung over—except Molly—and trying to enjoy the baby shower. Meg was exhausted by the pervasive, horrible acting alone.

When Edward called her cell, she was grateful for the chance to duck into Molly's home office to talk to him.

Immediately, her husband asked, "Did you get the photo I sent?"

"I got one this morning of all the kids watching a movie together. Is that what you mean?"

"Yeah. But you never answered." He sounded hurt.

"I'm sorry, babe," Meg said. "It was so sweet. I loved it, I swear." She'd been too busy keeping her big sister from hurling in their rental car to respond at the time, but who was counting?

"I thought we could frame it. Maybe send a copy home with your sister, too?"

"That's a great idea."

"Then what's wrong, love?" Edward asked. "You don't sound well. I'm worried about you."

"No, don't worry. Everything's fine, I promise." At least—they'd live, and that was essentially the same thing.

"Didn't you have fun last night?"

"It was…oh man, Edward, it was nuts. There was this brutal rum punch, and then a stripper showed up, and now we're all in agony, trying to play nice for this baby shower. I am too old for this crap," she confessed.

"Meg, darling, you're barely thirty. You aren't even kind-of old. Oddly, though, I could swear you just said a stripper showed up last night. A fact that tailors rather strangely with something my brother George was trying tell me on the phone, moments ago."

Meg groaned. "Oh, sweet mother of all that's holy. I completely forgot that I called Poppy last night. *What* was I thinking?"

Edward was chuckling, though. "Bit off a tad more than we could chew, eh?"

"I am so tired right now. You have no idea."

"Well…I have *some* idea. There's a video that sheds light on the subject, after all."

"I wish I was home right now. I just want to click my heels, have a hot bath, and crawl into bed with you. I may never come out again," Meg moaned.

"That sounds delightful. Shall I pencil you in for tomorrow, then?"

"Yes, please."

"Poor thing," he murmured. "Won't be long now, love. And then you'll be home with us, safe and sound. And we'll all breathe a bit easier, I think."

"Agreed. I'll call later to say goodnight to the girls."

Meg hated to hang up, but duty called. When she emerged from her hiding place, it was to find Stella clapping her hands officiously, proclaiming that it was time to open the gifts—even though they'd barely been socializing for an hour.

Each sharp, staccato burst of clapping registered like gunfire in Meg's still-sensitive eardrums…and based on the other expressions she saw around the room, she wasn't the only one. Elaine's Fun with Rum the night before had more than one woman papering over her misery with concealer, lipstick, and a fake smile she had to work too hard for.

They seemed to be missing one crucial element, though—the mother-to-be.

Elaine called loudly, "Molly! Where's Molly?"

Meg gave her a wave. "I'll find her," she said. Chances were high that her best friend was making a deposit with the porcelain gods, though they had to be getting tired of her version of tribute by now. Even so, Meg suspected the last person Molly would want intruding would be her mother.

The morning's honoree wasn't in the bathroom, however. Meg peeked around doorways and corners, and eventually discovered her in the dining room—folded into her husband's arms.

"One more day, sweet thing, and then we'll have this place to ourselves again," he murmured. Jake had wrapped his arms around Molly from behind and was smoothing his palms reverently over her large, round stomach.

"I never would've pegged you as being into whales," Molly snorted softly. "And frankly, I'm still not convinced you aren't faking."

"Woman, are you crazy? You're a goddess like this. Look at you—everywhere I touch, there's something hot to fill my hands with."

Meg cleared her throat quickly, before she invaded their privacy even more than she already had.

"There you are," she called.

The couple spun around, startled out of their marital moment.

"Sorry to interrupt," Meg explained. "But you're wanted in the other room."

Molly sagged and let out a heartfelt groan—she looked exhausted. She might not be hungover like the rest of them, but she'd told Meg earlier that she hadn't been sleeping well at night.

It couldn't be easy lugging that baby around all day, either. Molly had very likely overdone it the day before, trying to give her big sister the bachelorette party she thought Mina deserved.

Jake squeezed his wife's shoulders and laid his cheek against her hair.

"She's wanted here, too," he said.

"I have no doubt," Meg acknowledged. "But if we can get a few of those gifts opened, then the mamas will be appeased—and we can wrap this party up for good."

"Hmm. You drive a hard bargain," Molly said. "Which one of us is the lawyer, again?"

Jake said, "Just think, darlin'—if you power through this now, I'll bet you could be back in bed and sound asleep within the hour. I'll even rub your feet for you when you wake up."

Molly made a longing sound, and told Meg, "My feet hurt all the time. My back hurts, my knees hurt…"

"I know, Molls." Meg moved forward to take her by the hand, not liking how close Stella and Elaine's voices were getting. She pulled out one of the dining room chairs and pointed. "Sit down and take those ridiculous shoes off, first. You'll feel better. Then we'll get this thing over with."

Molly stuck a foot out and contemplated her admittedly-adorable wedges for barely a second before flopping down to comply. Jake crouched in front of her even faster—probably realizing that his wife would never be able to reach the buckles at her own ankles. Hell, he'd likely had to put the shoes on her to begin with.

Meg led her blissfully-shoeless friend back into the fray, and barely had Molly seated in the place of honor before the infernal doorbell was ringing again. When Elaine bolted for the foyer with a startled and dismayed exclamation, several faces registered apprehension.

Upon her return, Molly and Mina's mother exercised none of her excited fanfare from the evening before. She merely ushered the new arrival into the hushed family room, then stepped woodenly aside.

"Someone to see you, Molly," she announced.

More than one guest looked vaguely alarmed, and in the corner, Jake's great-aunt Ceecee sputtered a bit on her sip of tea—perhaps because the new arrival was a six-foot tall, white-feathered stork.

Or rather, a young woman *dressed* as a stork. Orange tights stretched over rail-thin legs, enormous, plush orange feet flopped across the hardwood floor…how did she walk in those things? Her costume was like a football mascot's—large and ungainly. Her arms were strapped to the underside of a pair of cape-like wings, and worst of all, a long, pointed orange beak protruded from the general area her chin ought to have been.

Meg had a sudden nonsensical moment of wondering what that plastic protuberance was reinforced with, given that a classic baby-bearing sling was dangling from it. There was no way a real baby could be in there, which begged the question—what *was?*

The performer couldn't have been more than eighteen or twenty. She paused on the threshold, and glanced uncertainly around the room at the shocked, assembled faces.

Meg saw Molly give the girl a sympathetic smile and nod. The girl cleared her throat, stepped forward, and burst into song.

You're having a baby,
Everyone is singing,
Maybe you're not ready,
But look what I am bringing!

Her voice was surprisingly rich and throaty, given her young age. When Meg noticed Shannon and Morgan swaying happily to the silly song, she thought the kid might have a real future as an R&B singer someday. Because, seriously, if she could make the next part work…

Samples and coupons,
Diapers and some jammies,

Everything you'll need,
Even a stuffed lamb-y!
…she was a musical genius. Molly and a few of the others began clapping, clearly assuming the song was over. Somehow, the stork-girl managed to navigate her considerable bulk around the furniture to deposit her bundle in Molly's lap—such as it was. She had one more message, though.

Just remember to call them,
All your friends and fam,
'Cause they can't wait to come and,
Lend a helping hand!
The stork finished her song with a far courtlier bow than should have been possible in her get-up, especially considering the truncated space she had to work with. A few errant feathers drifted to the floor in the ensuing silence.

Jake and Mack had been grinning as they watched the performance from the kitchen, but now Jake emerged to escort the girl to the door. Meg was tempted to follow—if only to determine if the actress intended to get behind the wheel of an actual car dressed like that.

Her steps stalled when she heard Mina's dry voice behind her, though.

"So…Mom. I'm assuming you're the one responsible for whatever that was?"

Molly looked up from the sack of baby paraphernalia in her lap. "Oh my God! I just realized—did you get a two-for-*one* deal?"

In the corner, Jake's grandmother let out an inelegant snort and was immediately shushed by Jake's mom.

Elaine glared at her daughter. "*No,* Smartypants, I didn't. They were from different companies. And for your information, I forgot about this one, all right?"

"I hope she didn't forget to *pay* her, too," Mina muttered in an aside that nearly every woman in the room heard.

"I handled it," hollered Jake, as he strolled back toward the kitchen. "She can settle with us later, if she wants."

"That boy is a prince," Ceecee told Shannon conspiratorially.

"You hear that, Molly?" Jake called, "I'm a prince. Better remember that the next time we run out of ice cream!"

Mina

HER MOTHER HAD somehow forgotten that she'd not only hired a skeevy stripper dressed as a construction worker, but *also* some girl dressed in a stork costume. Mina wouldn't have thought it possible, if she hadn't just witnessed the poor teenager singing her goofy song for them while they all sat stone-faced and clutching their mugs of coffee.

As Jake had ushered the stork out, Mina and the others stayed slumped in their seats. There was complete radio silence for a full drawn-out beat—but then, Healey started giggling and couldn't seem to stop…and her laugh was so infectious that everyone else was pretty much forced to chime in.

When Molly suddenly clapped a hand over her mouth and darted to the bathroom, they all simply laughed harder.

Their mother griped, "I *told* her not to eat all those cupcakes."

Before Mina could jump to her sister's defense, though, Molly's mother-in-law interjected, "Oh, stop. She wanted them. You've had babies—you know what that's like."

Sufficiently chastened, Elaine slunk into a chair in the corner, and Mina surveyed all the amused faces around the room. A warm sense of belonging settled over her. Against all odds, she'd somehow finally found her tribe.

Mina asked them, "Where have you people *been* all my life?"

Maybe they were all feeling a bit thin-skinned and sentimental after last night and that morning, but the only way she could describe what happened next, was to say that the room *erupted.*

Women all over the place were hugging each other and vowing their filial devotion.

Before long, Mina herself had broken down into sloppy crying, overwhelmed by the notion that she'd finally met some real girlfriends, on top of getting to be an aunt and a wife soon.

Molly emerged from the bathroom in tears, explaining to the party that it was mostly because she was hormonal, but also slightly due to being afraid that she might go into early labor from all the craziness…and what was more, the nursery wasn't done yet.

Elaine sobbed to Felice that she'd finally gotten to do all the things with her girls that she'd never had a chance to experience, and neither of them were the least bit grateful.

And Morgan and Meg tearfully bemoaned how much they missed their husbands and children and wanted to go home.

Mina mopped at her face with a soggy tissue, tried to take some deep breaths, and had to concede that perhaps the mimosas had been nearly as strong as that infamous rum punch.

Healey looked aghast at the watery display all around her. "What the heck is going on right now?" she asked.

"I have no idea," Shannon replied, "But I'm really hoping it's not contagious."

The response was both immediate and unified: "It is!"

THE FOLLOWING DAY, Mina and Mack were buckled into their airline seats and thousands of feet in the air, when he inquired, "Well, how was it? Are you glad you came?"

Mina smiled, "You have to ask?"

"You know kid, for a girl who claimed she had no female friends, you sure seem to be acquiring them at a breakneck pace," he told her.

Mina's smile edged into a grin. "I really am, aren't I?"

Mack hadn't joined her and Molly for their tearful send-off of the Flynn sisters earlier that morning, but he'd definitely noticed the way her phone had been chiming all day with contact information, photos, and inside jokes from most of the party guests.

"I'm happy for you, Mina. They all seem like really nice women," Mack told her.

"They are. I really like them."

"Good. Me too."

They paused to order drinks from the flight attendant, then Mina turned to study her fiancé.

"So…" She chewed on her lip, and felt an embarrassed heat creep up her neck. "You don't mind that I invited them all to our wedding? I don't know what got into me yesterday. It just sort of happened."

Mack laughed, "Of course, I don't mind. It'll be fun. Besides, I doubt adding another table or two to the reception is going to drag things out even worse. The place has room."

Mina drew circles on her drop-down tray with the condensation dripping off her can of juice. "I guess we should be thankful I didn't ask them all to be in the wedding, too. I almost did."

"Really?"

"Yeah…I was sitting there looking at how big Molly's belly has gotten and thinking there was no way she was going to be able to act as my matron of honor. I panicked a little."

"But you didn't pull the trigger?"

She shook her head. "No. I was afraid they'd think it was weird."

"That's okay, honey," he said. "Even if your sister can't do it, you'll still have my sisters, and Emily and Lilly to walk the aisle with you."

Mina warmed at the thought. Mack's younger twin sisters had been utterly ecstatic when she'd asked them to be bridesmaids. So much so, that Mina had been a little taken aback by it.

As for Emily, it'd been an impulse that had come out of nowhere, but Mina hadn't regretted it once since then. One minute, she was asking her friend Dimitri's daughter to be her flower girl…and the next, she'd gone and asked Dimitri's new girlfriend to be a bridesmaid, too. They *had* been spending a lot of time together, and Emily had turned out to be invaluable to have around, since Molly lived so far away.

"That's three bridesmaids and a flower girl, not counting Molly. Do you think that's enough?" Mina wondered. "People won't think it's lame, will they?"

Mack scoffed, "Who cares what people think? What matters is if you're happy with it."

As long as Mina got to tie the knot with the man beside her, she could be walking up the aisle with Elmer Fudd, and it wouldn't matter to her. She just didn't want to embarrass Mack in front of his family, that was all.

"They probably won't all come, anyway," she mused. "Shannon said she could be in trial, and Healey said her boyfriend might not be able to get the time off. And no way would Morgan come all the way back from New Zealand so soon."

"Why do you say that? Meg spent half an hour this morning talking about how her sister would bring us a wedding gift knitted from her sheep's wool, or something like that. I heard her myself. Why would she say that if she didn't mean it?"

"But it's so far. And Morgan barely knows me," Mina sighed.

"First of all, I don't think you can still say that, after the weekend you women just had. And secondly, I may or may not have heard Morgan on the phone with her husband, deciding whether they ought to stay in the U.S. a few weeks longer, just so they could make it."

Mina gawked at him. "Seriously?"

Mack nodded at her, eyes shining. "See? I told you she likes you."

She gnawed on her fingernail and counted heads to herself. "But…if they all show up and bring their dates, we could have another…eight people? Ten?"

Mack shrugged, unconcerned. "The more the merrier. If you're happy and you end up my legally-wed wife by the end of it, I don't care if you make friends with every woman on the Eastern seaboard in the next month." He waggled his eyebrows at her. "Hell, they can all babysit for us, too, as soon as I get you barefoot and pregnant."

A flight attendant passing by them in the aisle peeked curiously over, then quickly hurried away.

"*Mack*," Mina scolded. "Shh!"

"Listen you," he fired back. "You can't pretend like you've got no friends, because we both know that isn't true anymore. And I refuse to pretend like I'm not crazily, stupidly, obnoxiously in love with you, just to make some airline employee feel less jealous of my preposterous good fortune. I want to have babies with you, and I won't be silenced. So there."

"I love you," Mina replied, smiling at him.

"You'd better, or this is probably going to suck long term."

"*That's* what you come up with? *You'd better?*"

"You know how I feel about you, Mina," Mack said starchily. "I tell you all the damn time."

She poked him in the arm. "Then tell me again now."

"Bit bossy suddenly, aren't you?" He crossed his arms over his chest, and Mina admired the way it made his biceps bulge.

"Yes. I've been making all sorts of upgrades and improvements the past three days. Welcome to the new Mina," she intoned.

"That sounds ominous. And for the record, I liked old Mina just fine."

"*Liked?*" she sputtered.

"Yes. She was wonderful—kind and brave and great in the sack. Decent cook, too, as I recall."

"You know," Mina threatened. "I can drag out this engagement another six months if you want to play that game. Another *year*, even." She glared at him.

"*Shit*. No," Mack threw up his hands in defeat, then pivoted in his seat and used them to cup her cheeks. "I love you, New Mina.

As wide as the sky, and as vast as the world." He kissed her soundly, smack on the lips.

When she was eventually able to pull away, Mina conceded, "Now that's more like it."

Once, the future had felt like a harrowing, daunting thing. Not any longer though…now she was sailing into it with her head held high—part of a couple, and a member of a sisterhood. *Forever* looked sweet, and it started now.

Review

Did you enjoy **Forever and a Day**? If so, please consider leaving a review at the retailer where you purchased this title.

Book reviews can be as simple or as detailed as you wish, but all of them help authors sell more books, and assist other readers in finding the stories they want to read.

Almost any book can be reviewed by simply logging into the website where you purchased the title, then scrolling to the bottom of the title's product page to find an area called "Leave a Review."

Up Next

The Titan Was Tall

Triple Threat, Book One

Being in charge is a pain in the...

Posterior. Rear end. Junk in the trunk. Those were some of the words that came to mind when the captivating woman walked into Red's office that day. But now wasn't the time to contemplate her ass...ets. Red needed to focus on the fact that his huge conglomerate had just bought out her dinky publisher—and this sexy little author was the key to a smooth transition.

For all intents and purposes, Piper was his new star employee—so Red should not have cleared his schedule to take her dinner. He shouldn't have flirted like it was his freaking birthday, and he sure as hell shouldn't have gone and fallen for her. One more thing he shouldn't have done? Omit the fact that his company owed her a lot of money.

When his dirty little secret gets out, more than Red's new business acquisition is on the line—his jaded heart is hanging in the balance, too. Unfortunately, his golden way with a merger might not be enough to save him now.

Can Red convince Piper that her tentative trust in him wasn't misplaced? Or will their new relationship go the way of her missing royalties?

There's only one way to find out.

Step into his office and let Padraig "Red" MacLellan show you why he's the boss.

About the Series:
The three hot heroes of Triple Threat are primed to take Manhattan by storm, but there's one little problem...
Sometimes you win the girl, and sometimes she wins you.

The Titan Was Tall

One

IT WAS A bad time to develop a case of the nerves. Not that there was ever a good time, but developing the jitters when you were about to meet the person who could make or break your career did seem to be especially inconvenient.

Perhaps Piper was being dramatic. Her new overlord had merely contacted her lawyer a week ago, suggesting a perfectly civil "meet and greet" between Piper and the fearless leader. Perry had informed her that it wasn't the kind of suggestion one generally rebuffed, so here she was. She was sure there was nothing to worry about in the least.

PKM Industries—the conglomerate that had acquired her publisher several months earlier—had flown her up to New York for a three-day stay. They'd arranged for a driver to ferry her from the airport, installed her in a swanky hotel, and had even provided a generous meal stipend. They'd emailed an itinerary of who she was meeting with on each of the days, and assured Piper that it was not necessary to have her lawyer present. A good thing, too, since Perry was sharp and astute—but also somewhat…elderly.

Regardless, all the fuss didn't seem like the kind of thing they'd do if they were about to cut her loose. And why should they? Her books had sold well, almost from the moment she'd begun publishing. She would be a valuable asset to them.

However, Piper was not used to dealing with an enormous company with deep pockets. She'd been an author in Trident's stable for the entirety of her career, from the moment she'd graduated and submitted her first manuscript to an agent. And little

Trident was no juggernaut—just the labor of love of a kindly old couple who simply adored books and authors.

The Dentons weren't flashy, but they had been committed to the stories they sold. She'd been lucky to land with them. They had graciously helped her learn the industry and ensured that Piper did pretty well for herself. She owed them everything.

PKM was an entirely different kind of entity, though. As far as Piper knew, they rolled out the perks for every person they were about to sack. While it did seem as if the CEO could find someone a bit lower on the totem pole to do his firing for him, maybe he was just sadistic that way. Maybe he enjoyed it.

Piper fiddled with the buckle of her attaché case as the elevator chugged upward, and she tried not to let her worries get the best of her. She wasn't some green author who didn't know the ropes. She'd been doing this for eleven years and had the benefit of both a top-notch intellectual property lawyer and a reputable, experienced agent in her corner.

If this Padraig MacLellan guy was going to look at the work she'd done for Trident and decide to get rid of her, Piper would still land on her feet. Someone else would take her on because her fans would settle for nothing less. *She* would settle for nothing less.

She hoped it didn't come to that, though. It might be fun to see what she could accomplish with the resources of a larger company in the mix. She could expand her distribution, maybe, or get a few more translations of her backlist done. Maybe she could even work out a signing or two overseas. Who knew what PKM could do?

In the CEO's suite, she checked in with an extremely efficient young man named Wayne, dapper as a menswear ad in his gray plaid suit and pink dress shirt. He had clearly been waiting for her.

Wayne virtually leaped from his ergonomic chair to escort her straight to his boss, the estimable Padraig K. MacLellan. Or, as the tabloids claimed he was known, "Red." Piper straightened her spine as she stepped over his threshold, ready to do battle.

She was startled to discover that the head of the entire billion-dollar company was not an older, graying man, as she'd anticipated.

Okay, fine—she'd searched for him online, but this man wasn't the one whose picture she'd seen. This was a lion in his prime, preening in his lair.

The man who stood and rounded his large mahogany desk to greet her looked to be about her own age, tall and broad-shouldered, with thick, auburn hair and intense brown eyes. Piper's step hitched as she got closer. He was, in fact, larger than life—maybe 6'5 or more. He *loomed* over her. MacLellan was disconcertingly attractive, too, his grip firm but not bruising when they shook hands.

Wayne slipped discreetly out of the office, shutting the door behind him. Piper tried to ignore the way the touch of MacLellan's hand sent sparks up her arm, her nerve endings firing off a series of electric aftershocks that made her grateful for the large leather armchair he directed her to. She took an extra minute to arrange herself, locking down her composure while she was at it.

MacLellan eased into his own chair and smiled.

"Ms. Corelli," he began, "I'd like to thank you for coming up to see us. I hope your flight went okay?"

Had that been a royal *us*? "Yes, absolutely." Piper almost added, *thank you for having me*, but given how gorgeous MacLellan was, the phrase suddenly seemed laden with innuendo. She couldn't make herself utter it with a straight face.

"All the other accommodations to your liking? Hotel, and so forth?"

"Yes, of course. All of the arrangements have been lovely, thank you."

"That's a relief. My assistant can occasionally get creative with things like that."

"I see." Piper set her bag on the floor and folded her hands in her lap. She kept her knees together and crossed her ankles off to the side, infinitely decorous. She was a professional, but sometimes people got the wrong idea about her when they discovered she wrote erotic romances. Piper liked to do her level best to refute their assumptions.

Well, most of them at least. She wasn't going to go out of her way to hide her black lace tattoo, curving around her ankle. And she certainly wasn't going to attend a meeting of this magnitude without wearing her lucky shoes—which happened to be four-inch, leopard-printed calf-hair peep-toes. She *was* a romance writer. Come on.

"It says here you live in Maryland?"

"That's right."

"I've never been. What's it like?"

"Well…I'd say it has a bit of everything. Within a two-hour radius, you can find city and farmland, skiing, sailing—you name it."

"Sounds fascinating. How could I have missed that?"

"Ah, well. Something for your bucket list," she tossed off casually. Oh, yeah. She was cool as cool could be. MacLellan would never guess what she was going through.

He laid his hands on his desk, and Piper immediately noticed his long, elegant fingers. He stared absently at her, a slight furrow forming between his eyebrows, and she agonized over what he might be thinking.

She cleared her throat. "Let's get started."

"Forgive me," he muttered. "It's been one hell of a week." He shuffled some papers around and refocused on her. "Let's, uh—let's start over."

"I'd be delighted. But I must admit, I'm not entirely clear why I'm here right now."

A small smile quirked up one corner of his mouth, turning him even more roguishly handsome. "Maybe I can enlighten you." He reached for a file laying to the side of his desk, centered it in front of him, and flipped it open.

"Ms. Corelli, when we acquired Trident Publishing—"

Piper held up a hand to stop him. "I'm sorry to interrupt. I just wanted to make sure you realized that 'Antoinette Corelli' is my pen name. My real name is Piper Fulham."

MacLellan shuffled a couple of pages around, read one with a frown, and peered back up at her. "Piper Mae Fulham. So it is. I overlooked that. I apologize, Piper Mae." His mouth twisted slightly.

Piper waved him off. "Happens all the time. And please, just Piper is fine."

"Excellent." He waited to make sure she had nothing further to add, then proceeded, "When we acquired Trident and started really combing through the nuts-and-bolts of how to stabilize it, we came across some surprising details. Maybe you already know."

The former owners of Trident might have loved books, but they weren't exactly business-savvy sharks. Piper was not at all surprised to hear the company wasn't up to this man's standards, so she simply nodded politely.

"I'd already reviewed the industry, and I knew that eBooks were major drivers. But," the CEO continued, "I was fascinated to discover that the highest grossing segment of this company was its romance division." He glanced up at her from the papers spread in front of him, allowing that tidbit to settle.

Piper sat patiently and refused to pity him. He ought to have known that, but no matter. *She* knew what she did for a living, and why it mattered so very much to people. Love truly did make the world go around.

"And who, amidst that whole division," he asked, "would you guess was earning us more money than any other author?" He consulted his notes, then elaborated, "More than the next four authors combined, to be precise."

Piper smiled thinly. Oh, she knew all right. The Dentons had made no secret of the fact. "Why don't you tell me?"

MacLellan ignored her little flash of smugness. "I will. It's you. Your books alone appear to have kept afloat an entire, wildly-mismanaged publishing house that was hemorrhaging money from nearly every other line of business."

"I've been very fortunate," Piper agreed.

"It seems so. But…I will admit to having felt some chagrin at never having *heard* of you before. Not one media profile, not one article, not one book review. Not even a whisper of your name crossed into my purview."

Well, he didn't have to be quite so emphatic about it. "You aren't exactly my target audience," Piper pointed out wryly. Though he'd make an excellent character study.

MacLellan sat back and regarded her carefully. "I'm not so sure about that."

"You're not?" The dissonance between their actual conversation, versus the one transpiring in her head, was throwing her completely off-kilter. She had to pull herself together before she missed something important.

"No. Because once it became clear that I had never heard of my highest-selling author before, I also realized that I'd never cracked open a single romance novel of any kind before. That kind of ignorance does not sit well with me, so naturally, I set about educating myself."

"You didn't." This interview was taking a decidedly unexpected turn, and Piper didn't have a clue where it was headed next. Was this guy some kind of holy roller, about to tell her all the ways her books were paving the way for the devil's work? Or was he about to get skeevy on her?

"I most certainly did," MacLellan assured her. "First, I read the current releases of several chart-topping authors at other publishing houses. Next, I sampled what some of the bigger indie writers had to offer. Laying some groundwork, if you will."

Piper watched him, trying to get a read on his expression, but it was impossible. "And?" she prompted.

"*And*," he said, "then I read yours."

"I see," Piper replied, though she didn't.

He asked, "Do you? Because once I read one, it seemed like maybe I should read another. From there, it definitely snowballed—pretty quickly, too. Took me a month and a half, but I read them."

"Which, uh…which ones?" Piper's mind was spinning with scenes from some of her more risqué stuff, mixing in some very unhelpful images of the man before her *reacting* to them. As one of her characters might say, *Oh, God.*

MacLellan made a show of checking his report once more. "All of them," he reported.

"In a month and a half?" Piper blurted. That was no small feat.

Her new employer's mouth twitched up at the corners again. "I found them very compelling."

"Clearly," Piper laughed, but it was thin and nervous-sounding.

He waited for a full beat, then two. Watching her. Waiting. She gazed back and tried to school her breathing. There was no hope for her heart rate, though.

"Forgive me," he said. "I've flustered you."

Crud. Not only was MacLellan smoking hot, but he was perceptive, too. Worse, he appeared to be one of those uncomfortable conversationalists who felt the need to drag awkwardness out into the open and shine a light on it.

For an introvert like her, that made him virtually a monster. If she'd learned anything, though, it was how to be a good faker. Her whole image depended on it.

When she replied, "What makes you say that?" it was blasé. So convincing.

He didn't respond directly. Instead, MacLellan inquired, "Was it me veering into odd superfan territory that did it, or was it just my unnaturally large size?"

Piper couldn't help it. Her eyes flicked down toward his lap, hidden behind that colossal, weighty desk, for only an instant before she wrenched them back up to his face in a panic. She blinked rapidly, plum out of snappy comebacks.

MacLellan's mouth stayed serious, but now his eyes twinkled with laughter. "It's okay. I like to get out in front of the elephant in the room, so to speak, so we can get past it. I realize that I'm a tad too enormous to be considered normal. I make people uncomfortable. Especially ones of your stature," he mused.

Piper could feel her face flaming. No way could he read her mind, but did he have any conception of how dirty he sounded? She had to get her mind out of the gutter. Piper decided to feign indignation at the height jab, if only as a deflection.

"Now wait just one minute," she muttered, then winced at her tone. Her voice was too freaking breathy to sound anything but flirtatious.

"I'd like to say that I'm a gentle giant to make up for it, but then I'd be lying to you within five minutes of meeting you, and that hardly seems sporting." Then the bastard winked. *Winked.*

Piper nearly swallowed her tongue. What the hell was happening here? Was he flirting *back*?

"I'm sure you're a perfectly fine person, towering or not," she managed. If MacLellan was a perfectly *proportioned* person, issues with endowment would not be a problem for him. But she was Not. Going to. Dwell on that. For crying out loud.

"Anyway." The head of PKM cleared his throat and shifted his gaze to the side, looking thoughtful. "It goes without saying that hanging on to you—particularly through this transition phase—is imperative for Trident. I wanted to meet with you face-to-face to get your thoughts on that, as well as to deliver this new contract to you." His eyes, when they returned to her, were a deep brown, like chocolate.

Piper took the packet and flipped absently through the first few pages. Numbers jumped out at her, and she felt her eyebrows notch upward.

"I…have no current plans to leave Trident," she said. Not now, anyway.

He chuckled—a low, delectable sound. "I'm relieved to hear that."

Quickly, she added, "But naturally, I'll need to review this with my attorney before I sign it."

MacLellan smiled wider. "Of course. That copy is yours. We'll forward another to your lawyer and let them know when we need it back." He shuffled through his file. "Perry Shanahan, correct?"

Piper nodded, and he began gathering the papers on his desk, arranging them neatly back into their file. All the facts and figures breaking down her career, her passion, and who knew what else for him—all encased in their slim, brown cardstock folder. If only her real life could be arranged so easily.

Their meeting was clearly at an end. Piper wondered briefly if MacLellan would be sitting in on any of the others she had scheduled, but decided that would be more of a nuisance than anything else.

She slipped her new contract into her bag. "Thank you for this, and for taking the time to meet with me personally. I appreciate the effort," she began. Though not as much as she planned to appreciate some of those zeroes she'd spotted in the new contract. PKM wasn't messing around.

"Of course," he said. Then, like he really could read her mind, he added, "I have no doubt the other meetings Wayne set up for you will go equally smoothly."

In the next couple of days, Piper would be talking to employees who would have a far more direct influence on her career—PKM's new editors, cover designers, and audiobook performers. Getting used to an unfamiliar crew would be an adjustment, but they could hardly be more difficult than the disorganized set-up she'd had to deal with before.

"I'm sure they will." She would probably never lay eyes on this man again. It would be insane for him to get involved in Trident's business at such a microscopic level. She frankly couldn't believe he'd even gone through with this meeting.

"You're heading back to Maryland afterward, I assume?"

"Yes." Piper set her bag in her lap and prepared to stand. Now that her uneasiness had mostly subsided, she was realizing that she'd never eaten lunch. She was hungry and more eager than ever to get out of there so she could go find something to eat.

MacLellan drummed his fingers on her file. "Any other plans while you're here?"

Again, Piper tried not to notice what great-looking hands the man had, but it was hard. Noticing superior male traits like that, then writing about them to perfection, was kind of her jam.

His wrists were oddly tantalizing, too—tan and lean where they peeked out from the starched white cuffs of his dress shirt.

"No," she blurted abruptly, then added sheepishly, "Not really." By way of explanation, she tacked on, "I wasn't sure what I'd have time for." Right. Not lame at all.

MacLellan contemplated that information, then seemed to make a decision. "Listen." He hesitated, then plowed on with a determined look, "You're my last appointment of the day. Why don't we grab some dinner?"

"I…that's not necessary," Piper stuttered out. "I'm sure my hotel has a restaurant downstairs." She tried to picture it but came up blank. "Or something." There was a bar, she knew that for sure. "The front desk can direct me somewhere, either way. Or, I can just get room service." And why was she rambling, exactly?

MacLellan stood behind his desk and reached to shut down his laptop. He looked amused, and warmer than he'd been. "I'm fairly confident that I can do better than room service if you're amenable. What do you say? Do you trust me?"

The giant of the business world was gone, replaced by a smiling, friendly man who was too toweringly handsome for anyone's peace of mind.

Piper would be no kind of romance author at all if she turned down the chance to study him a little longer. Opportunities like this one, needless to say, were a bit thin on the ground where she lived. She suspected by the end of a meal with this man, she'd have good ideas for a new character, a new story—heck, a whole steamy new series.

"Yeah," she replied, trying to focus. "Sure."

MacLellan came around the desk and led her out of his office, locking his door behind him. His hand was a barely-there hint of warmth at her lower back. When they passed his assistant's desk, Wayne popped out of his chair like an agitated preschooler.

"Where—" he began.

"Clear my schedule," MacLellan instructed blandly. "I'm leaving for the day. Could you ring down for the car?"

His startled assistant sank back into his seat. "Okay," he said. Wayne glanced at his monitor with a wild, desperate sort of look. "What should I—"

"Handle it," MacLellan ordered.

Piper got a glimpse of his assistant diving for his phone when MacLellan ushered her out, and then the office door swung shut, blocking her view.

As they reached the bank of elevators, Piper turned to her companion. "Last appointment of the day, huh?"

"Yup," he grinned.

She had to laugh. "Mr. MacLellan—"

"Call me Red."

"Okay, Red. Why are you doing this?"

He chuckled, handing her into the elevator and then pressing the button for the lobby. "Curiosity?"

"If that's true, prepare to be underwhelmed," she told him. She'd discovered the hard way that the reality of a romance novelist simply couldn't live up to the hype.

The doors closed, surrounding them in gleaming brass and mirrors on all sides. Piper swallowed against her sudden hyperawareness of Red, his height and intoxicating male scent. And, *damn* it, she had to stop thinking like she was writing. This man was not one of her heroes. He was her *boss*.

Red's eyes flickered down, apparently snared by what should have been the imperceptible motion of her throat. It was just long enough for Piper to glimpse his lashes, and quite long enough for her heart to lurch alarmingly in her chest.

And then it was over, and he was smiling at her again. Awareness went both ways, it seemed.

"Hungry?" Red inquired. His voice was dark. Seductive. It was as if they'd traveled to an alternate, far-sexier plane of existence when they'd entered this shining little box.

You have no idea, Piper thought.

"Always," she said aloud, and the blasted man went and laughed.

"Do you have any preferences? Likes, dislikes, that sort of thing?" Red studied her in that unnerving way of his, as if he could discern her answer just by looking hard enough.

"I can find something to eat almost anywhere," Piper hedged. "I'm not terribly particular, I'm afraid."

She took in his raised eyebrow and slightly annoyed look and sighed. So, indecision wasn't going to work.

"Okay, fine," she said. "I especially like Japanese, Italian, and Mexican food. Does that help?"

"Much better."

He smelled ridiculously good. It wasn't fair. She asked, "Do you know a good place?"

"I know the best place," he said smugly.

"Then I am very much in favor, kind sir."

His scent infused the enclosed space, drifting around her, and clearly making her crazy. Piper knew this for a fact, because her next words were, "Do you mind if I ask what cologne you're wearing?"

Oh, God.

She stumbled on, "I'm sorry. I only ask because I'm very sensitive to smells, and I don't often enjoy perfume. I noticed yours and it's…"

Piper could almost hear the sound of the shovel as she dug a deeper and deeper hole for herself. Nerves. This was only nerves. Once they were out of this infernally small space, she'd be better.

Red looked uncomfortable and checked the floor numbers flickering over the elevator door. "Forgive me. Is it bothering you?"

"No! No," Piper assured him. "Actually, I'm surprised by how much I like it."

At another arch look from him, she appended lamely, "Usually I don't."

Red's concern morphed immediately into an amused smirk. "Are you telling me I smell good, Miss Fulham?"

"Great. The word you want is *great*."

He chuckled, and her heart pounded harder. Mercifully, the elevator door slid open on the ground floor, saving her from making an even bigger ass out of herself.

The doorman wished them a good afternoon, Red whisked her across the sidewalk, and then he opened the back door of a sleek black sedan idling at the curb. When Piper moved past him to enter, she felt the warm whisper of his breath near her ear. She turned in confusion to find him very close indeed.

He grinned, unapologetic. "Turns out you smell great, too."

To read more, please purchase *The Titan Was Tall* from your favorite bookseller!

FREE BOOK

Get a glimpse of Morgan, Meg, Molly and Mina—*before* their happily ever afters take place!

Sign up for the author's Reader's List and get a free copy of the Lost & Found prequel novella "Girls Night Out."

Visit Here to Get Started:

http://eepurl.com/ctGk1j

Also by Kristen Casey

The Triple Threat Series

The Titan Was Tall

The Doctor Was Dark

The Hero Was Handsome

The Masquerade was Magic

The Hero's Brother

The Triple Threat Box Set

The Black Watch Security Series

False Flag

Heat Seeking Missile

Brothers in Arms

Fight or Flight

Search and Destroy

Squared Away

Acknowledgements

Each of the books in the Lost & Found series has been something of a group effort. While I was writing them, I continuously ran ideas by my friends and family, wondering if my imagination had "jumped the shark" once and for all. I'm grateful that they humored me in those instances and treated the majority of those conversations as if they were perfectly normal.

Thanks go to my editor and beta-reader Helen, who may be the best listener on Earth—in addition to a sharp-eyed finder of errors and relentless enemy of inconsistencies. Plus, she laughs at my jokes, so it's easy to see why she's indispensable.

Many thanks also go to Deborah at Tugboat Design for her beautiful cover. She's a true professional and a genuinely nice person, and I'm so fortunate I found her out in that vast abyss known as the internet.

To my family I can only say, you guys are my greatest accomplishment—better than any book I've ever read or written. The faith you put in me makes me a better person every day, and I love you more than you'll ever know. Now, for crying out loud, get off your devices and go do your chores.

About the Author

Kristen Casey writes the kind of heartfelt, steamy books she loves to read—full of relatable characters and delicious dialogue. She lives in Maryland with her husband, kids, and assorted cats, and in her free time, she enjoys all things crafty—especially projects she finds on Pinterest.

Sign up for her newsletter to receive exclusive free content and the inside scoop on sales and new releases—all emailed right to your inbox.

You can also follow her on social media for behind-the-scenes tales, character and setting inspiration, book reviews, and more:

Goodreads: Kristen_Casey
Facebook: AuthorKCasey
Twitter: AuthorKCasey
Pinterest: KristenCase0461
Instagram: Kristen.Casey.Books
BookBub: Kristen Casey
TikTok: KristenWritesRomance

Reading Order of Kristen's Books

The Lost & Found Series

Girls Night Out (Prequel exclusive to subscribers)

Finding Home (Book 1)

Finding Love (Book 2)

Lost in Love (Book 2.5—Includes *Lucky in Love*)

The Flynn Sisters Box Set (Includes *Christmas in Cambridge*)

Finding a Husband (Book 3)

Finding Forever (Book 4)

Forever and a Day (Book 4.5—Includes *Forever Starts Now*)

The O'Connell Sisters Box Set (Includes *Heroes & Husbands*)

The Triple Threat Series

The Titan was Tall (Book 1)

The Doctor was Dark (Book 2)

The Hero was Handsome (Book 3)

The Triple Threat Box Set (Includes *The Masquerade was Magic* and *The Hero's Brother*)

The Black Watch Security Series

False Flag (Book 1)

Heat Seeking Missile (Book 2)

Brothers in Arms (Book 3)

Fight or Flight (Book 4)

Search and Destroy (Book 5)

Squared Away (Book 6)